NORTHERN STORIES
Volume Five

NORTHERN STORIES
Volume Five

Edited by Beryl Bainbridge and David Pownall

1994

Published by Arc Publications
Nanholme Mill, Shaw Wood Road
Todmorden, Lancs. OL14 6DA

Copyright © remains with the authors 1994

ISBN 0 946407 97 5

Design and print by Arc & Throstle Press
Shaw Wood Road, Todmorden, Lancs. OL14 6DA

The Publishers acknowledge financial assistance
from Yorkshire and Humberside Arts Board and
North West Arts Board.

CONTENTS

Preface by Beryl Bainbridge and David Pownall 7

Addy Farmer The Devil You Know 9
Howard Baker Market Forces 16
Adrian Wilson Quite a Night, Darling 24
Richard J. Hand Landlord and Lodger 28
Johanna Fawkes Et in Arcadia Ego 34
Stuart Allison The Gate 43
Ian Smith Jereminsky's Oranges 50
Grace Harvey Dead Man's Shoes 57
Stephen G. Holden When Harriet Returns 64
Robert Graham Carcasses 69
Gary Webb The Strange Case of Marie Annette 75
Kathleen Jones Glass 80
Stephen Bohl Dinosaur 85
Wendy Robertson Passion 94

The Contributors 101
The Editors 104
Shortlist 105

PREFACE

A year or so back, the novelist Francis King and I took part in a discussion on the "short story". We were asked to name our favourite titles. I chose *Christ in Concrete, Cinderella* and *The Monkey's Paw*. Mr. King put as his first choice Joseph Conrad's *Heart of Darkness*.

A novelist is expected, if not obliged, to expand his narrative beyond two hundred pages; a poet, should he wish, is at liberty to express himself in less than eight lines. The story writer, dangling between the two extremes, has the most difficult task of all, given that in these days length is dictated by the amount of columns available in the very few journals still catering to the genre; anything in excess of four thousand words is considered to be over-long. Thus the modern short story, curtailed by lack of space, must engage the reader from first to last paragraph. There isn't time for development of character or atmosphere; language and plot are essential.

As far as David Pownall and myself were able, we tried to pick for this volume those pieces which seemed to fit this criteria. We think we chose pretty well, and found enormous pleasure in reading the work of so many northern writers. Had the finished book run to more pages, two dozen more stories would have been included.

That great man of the movies, Samuel Goldwyn, is reported to have told some unfortunate script-writer, "What we want is a story that starts with an earthquake and works its way up to climax".

It may be a bit vulgar, commercially speaking, but there's a worm of truth in the apple.

Beryl Bainbridge

To read nearly two hundred short stories in a fortnight of hot summer weather is an oddly unnorthern experience. Judgement becomes increasingly subjective (detachment is plant of cool climates) and the common human themes build into a Hallelujah Chorus rolling round the garden air. By the time I reached the last story I was stuck with the belief that memorability was all. What else made a story survive? And how does this memorability work? It nags, it sticks, it tickles, it provokes, it produces sorrow or laughter, and much of its art is secret and hidden.

Beryl and I found a high degree of accord on eight of the stories. One of my top personal choices – *The Search* by Ken Lickley – was disqualified because it exceeded the limit for length by 467 words. Let this be a lesson to anyone who doubts that accountancy is more important than talent. I hope that Ken Lickley will have enough black humour left from writing his story not to be discouraged by this disappointment.

David Pownall

Addy Farmer

The Devil You Know

I saw the devil for the first time when I was six. Except that then I did not know it was the devil, not until my grandmother put me right. She was always on the lookout for the devil, who could strike anywhere and at any time and she did not want me to go the way of our family. I was vulnerable she said, I was innocent and that's how he likes them, naive and stupid about the world.

I remember this much else. It was hot and I was bored. We had come for a day out in York with my grandmother and I was sulking. I wanted to see inside Clifford's Tower and to walk along the walls and look down on the city. My grandmother was all for that idea but my parents wanted to visit the shops. There was a promise of Betty's for tea and cakes, but it seemed a lifetime away. We waited endlessly for my parents outside big, busy shops, my grandmother's hand sticky around mine. She was looking this way and that, her face flushed and dewy in the red heat. I thought she looked a hundred years old and I stared at her, willing her to look down. I wanted to ask her what she was looking for, why she always looked away, out of windows, through doors, over walls. She was so anxious today that when my parents emerged, she grasped thankfully at my father's arm; she still loved him then.

It was then that I slipped away. Away from my grandmother's sweaty palmed protection in the direction of a stomping, thumping drum and bells, an urgent tantalising sound which crashed its way through the still heat and pulled me in its wake. I had to find it and I pushed my way through the mass of people swelling in front of me. They were all looking ahead, staring at a rhythmic procession which swayed soundlessly to the insistent music. It was a procession of devils, searching with soulless eyes behind their still, smooth masks. Of course the man just in front of me thought, as I did at the time, that they were merely the Open Air Theatre Company from Bradford but I should have guessed. The devils were dressed monstrously and mesmerically in single flowing colours of red, white, gold and black. They danced grotesquely on their tottering wooden legs. They menaced the crowd with their elongated talons and their dead, alien heads. I was hoisted up onto the shoulders of the stranger in front of me and I could see that though they all wore different colours, their eyes were all the same empty black. The devils were stopping occasionally, bending low like predatory insects

10 / *The Devil You Know*

and demanding money from their captive audience. The man gave me fifty pence and I waved it around, not wanting to attract their attention but unable to stop myself. I was lost and the devils knew it. Two of the nearest seemed to sniff the air like dogs and then, at a crash of symbols, the red devil strode towards me. I held my money out to him, stretching my arms as far as they could go. The black eyes danced to the music, the talons waved and beckoned and I was ensnared, the devil was coming to fetch me. That is until the world fell down, when my father wrenched me backwards from the stranger's shoulders and the devil in front of me seemed to shrink and disappear in a billow of red. I was gathered away from the scene by my parents. I could hear some shouting and shrieking but I was safe. My mother took me to Betty's and told me that I should not trust strangers and I thought it strange at the time that she should be more concerned for my body than for my soul. It was only after my second chocolate éclair that my father arrived with my grandmother. She gave me a great hug and whispered that I was safe from the devil today. I saw my parents exchange glances. Yes, said my grandmother smiling with satisfaction as she sat down, the police had been very understanding when she explained that she had had to saw the devil's leg off; after all she was only protecting her grandson.

Of course, after that, my grandmother had told me everything about the family secret. How generations of our young men had fallen under the devil's influence and whistled their souls away. I wondered about this and determined never to master whistling or listen to another one of my parents' Roger Whittaker records. I worried about my parents but my grandmother said that it may be too late for them already. Her duty now was to save me from the devil; but, said my grandmother, winking slyly, he has to find you first. From then on I decided that my grandmother's small world was the best protection from the devil. Inside her dark cottage within that tiny village all seemed safe. My parents did not seem to mind and would drop me off there every weekend, waving cheerily, their car loaded down with suitcases and the paraphernalia of travelling. As to my grandmother, she barely acknowledged them but hustled me into the cottage looking over my head and then sighing with relief as she closed the door. Once inside, she made me drink what she called a cleansing tea, which tasted disgusting but I accepted as part of the protective ring she was drawing around me.

The Devil You Know / 11

My grandmother was always busy researching into the ways and means of Satan – better the devil you know than the devil you don't, she would mutter – and as the years went by, the cottage floor became increasingly lost under unruly piles of books and manuscripts. Eventually Mrs. Rogers, the cleaner who came in once a week, resigned, saying it wasn't natural. It fell to me to keep my grandmother in some sort of order and so, by the age of twelve, I was buying her basic foodstuffs from the local post office. This was unfortunate since their range was somewhat limited and our staple weekend diet was a can of Argentinian ratatouille or a Fray Bentos pie. My grandmother did have a car but I had never seen her use it. It did not matter. I knew that my grandmother would never travel to somewhere like York again; by then I realised that these cities were too full of the world and beyond the control of God.

It came as quite a surprise to my parents that I was missing school to go and look after my grandmother. It caused quite a row, especially when the social services threatened to step in. I said that I didn't care for school and that I was learning everything I needed to learn from my grandmother. My father said I learnt a good deal of the wrong thing at her house and that she was a wicked old woman who had stolen their son away. I pointed out that they seemed quite happy for her to steal me when it suited them and we were all silent for a while. I could hear the devil laughing outside the window and it terrified me. I wanted to run back to the safety of my grandmother's tiny cottage but my parents held me within their evil eye. I was trapped. I retreated into silence, what was there to say? I could not trust my parents anymore. They thought that I did not notice their askance dark looks and their kitchen mutterings, but I did. I would telephone my grandmother when they had gone to bed and she gave me the recipe for her cleansing tea and advised me to hide in their wardrobe to find out their doings. This I did, and heard evil words about my grandmother and talk of sending me to a boarding school away from her influence. I head a lot more besides, frightening sucking and clamping noises. When I told my grandmother, she said they were communing with the devil and that I should pray hard to God for protection until she came up with a solution.

Life became a constant battle to ward off the advances of the devil. Instead of doing my homework, I would spend hours praying

12 / *The Devil You Know*

that my grandmother would come and take me away. Then one night she invited herself round for supper. My parents pretended to be pleased to see her and offered her something fizzy from a green bottle. I was relieved to see that she was not fooled by this and, winking at me, tipped the evil drink onto the carpet when their backs were turned. As it was, my parents had something to tell her, something they thought would make her very happy. They were expecting a baby. I was shocked. They were so old, it was obscene. My grandmother's valiant effort to conceal her disgust finally broke down and she threw her glass at the wall, shouting spawn of Satan. My mother ran from the room and my father went red in the face and told me to go to bed. I turned to my grandmother and she motioned for me to leave, making the sign of the cross in the palm of her hand. I could hear my mother upstairs, wailing and gnashing her teeth and so I went outside into the cool night air. For some reason I felt excited. This was it, this was the showdown between good and evil; after tonight nothing would ever be the same. I knew that I no longer wished to live with my parental parasites who were sucking the goodness out of me. My grandmother suddenly flew out of the front door and, spotting me, whispered to me to be patient and pray, she would be the instrument of my liberation. I went back indoors and saw my father kneeling on the floor sponging the wet patch on the carpet. He muttered shocking devilish words about his own mother, incontinent, senile, evil, bonkers. I could not bear to hear anymore and fled upstairs.

Anyway, God looks after his own. That very next day at school I was summoned to Mrs. Beatty's office where my grandmother was also present. They both looked very solemn but I caught the wink my grandmother gave me and was cheered. It turned out that my parents had been killed in a car accident on some notorious stretch of bypass. Mrs. Beatty gave me a handkerchief and told me to let my grief out, that they were all here to help me. Then I did cry, but it was with the pent up pain of a prisoner who has finally been given release. Now I would be safe and I glanced with relief at my grandmother who looked back with dry twinkling eyes.

For a while I lived in the potting shed as part of the cleansing process. This I understood. I did not want to contaminate the house with any residual evil and it was not for very long. My days at school became more and more infrequent as the world pressed in on us with increasing intensity and my grandmother's fears and

The Devil You Know / 13

needs became more urgent. The need to define the nature of the evil that threatened us was paramount now. She could feel the devil drawing nearer, she said, and in the darkest deep of the night I thought I could hear his distant laughter. I still had to go to the local library to collect my grandmother's obscure book orders but I always made sure that I was back at the cottage by dusk. We had all our food delivered to the house from the large grocery store in the next town; we had no need to worry about the cost since the deaths of my parents. I thought it was a shame that we could not have Mrs. Rogers back to help us but my grandmother suspected that she might be the devil's disciple. In fact it turned out that most of the village were veering in the direction of Satan and that only the vicar might be exempt from his influence.

So it was not until I was sixteen that I met an angel. I went to the library somewhat later than usual on that afternoon in early summer. I was picking up a paper my grandmother had ordered called 'The Devil Speaks and I Will Listen'. I fumbled for the order slip as I came in through the heavy wooden door, anxious to be away. I found it and as I looked up I was startled by goodness made flesh. She was a serene Titian beauty with a sky blue smile, the last lingerings of which were bestowed on me as she turned to help me. For the first time in my life I experienced a vague sense of embarrassment about my grandmother. How could I ask this untainted creature to touch words of evil? But she took the order slip without a trace of shock and returned with the paper. She smiled again as she handed it over and somewhere in the very back of beyond in my mind I heard the creak of a door opening on rusty hinges.

I could not hide anything from my grandmother. I had been too long away, something had happened, she could sense it she said. I was about to tell her about the angel when she rushed away to the kitchen, to make, she said, a double dose of her cleansing tea to rid me of any aura of evil. I was shocked. It was not true. My grandmother had to be wrong. I waited until her back was turned and then I poured the brew onto the pot plant I had bought my grandmother for her birthday. I went to bed that night feeling desperately uneasy but for once I did not dream of the devil but of something as yet beyond my grasp. I went out early the next day and went straight to the library. She was there, she was not a dream. She was talking to the other librarian and her voice was musical.

14 / *The Devil You Know*

She saw me and I turned too hastily and began rifling through Thomas the Tank Engine. Miranda, I heard the other librarian say. Miranda, it was perfect for her. Over the next few weeks I haunted the library, mesmerized by Miranda. I ceased to drink my grandmother's cleansing tea or listen to her warning words. I just went through the motions of eating, drinking and praying. Eventually the pot plant died. It was that, I think, which gave the game away to my grandmother, that sour drooping death. I know that she did not mean to do what she did, that she was only trying to protect me but it sent me running into the arms of the devil all the same.

That morning I felt more alive than I had ever done. That morning I had spoken to Miranda and that morning she had agreed to go walking with me. How could I not tell the person whom I loved more than anyone else in the world? How could I anticipate that my grandmother would not share in my total joy, that she would twist my happiness into something quite other? She did not speak at first but turned her head to the place where the pot plant had stood and fell onto her knees and began to pray fervently for the deliverance of my soul from the clawing grip of the devil's helper, Miranda. It was then that I began to suspect that my grandmother might just be a little mad and I ran from the house and to the church where I prayed for help.

I met Miranda at seven thirty that evening outside the library. She was wearing a light blue cotton dress and she smiled her gorgeous smile as I approached her. We talked and we talked as we walked alongside the stream in the water meadow. We bought fish and chips and sat eating them, idly sitting on a bench on the green and then Miranda took me for a drink in The Beamish Bear. No-one questioned us, we were both tall for our ages and Miranda had been in there before. We took our drinks outside and it would have been perfect had my grandmother not appeared. She was quite spectacular, that I will say for her. She descended from the car park in cloud of avenging white material which looked suspiciously like the sitting room curtains. For an elderly lady she moved with astonishing speed and ferocity but it was the strength of righteous madness. She drove the cake knife home three times before any one of the astonished onlookers could stop her. Blood soaked the white gown and spattered across the blue of Miranda's dress. The red billowed away from me and as I sank, I saw the horrified look in Miranda's eyes. I held onto her hands and closed my eyes, resting my head in her angel's lap. I heard the devil chuckle and saw the empty black eyes of my grandmother. The devil had me at last but I had already touched heaven.

Howard Baker

Market Forces

The alarm shrieked at 8 a.m. and even before Haley hauled himself out of bed he knew it was going to be one of those days. The sight of his breath drifting mistily towards the ceiling indicated that the previous day's power cut had snaffled the central heating timer, and the sound of gunfire rising from the street beyond his window suggested that the milk would be late getting through. The feeling of depression was compounded by lack of sleep; in the early hours the anti-theft device on his car had activated and he had achieved only a fitful doze after the echoes of the detonation faded.

Dragging on his clothes he lurched shivering to the window and peered through the loophole in the metal shutters. As he had guessed, the regular milkman was pinned down by a sniper; his gaily-coloured float was slewed across the street and muzzle-flashes indicated that he had sought refuge beneath it. Haley squinted against the weak April sunlight but failed to locate the opposition. He did, however, note the blasted carcass of his car lying crumpled on the verge opposite. A smudge of smoke filtered languidly from the charred interior, blurring the detail of the two figures stretched out on the ground beside it. He would have to settle for black coffee and a taxi.

He washed and shaved hurriedly, located his mobiphone and after dialling a dozen times secured a signal that was not jammed into crackling incoherence by one or other of the competing telephone companies. Having ordered a car he wandered through to the kitchen, brewed coffee and punched the radio. A tanker was aground in the Channel and bids to rescue the crew were invited by the owner's accountants. The head of BritAir had denied that the secret purchase of ground-to-air missiles was part of a strategy designed to give his airline a monopoly. Research by the country's largest CD manufacturer had revealed vinyl albums to be a major cause of cancer. The interminable war in former Yugoslavia had been temporarily suspended while the opposing factions sought to discover who they were currently fighting . . . It sounded like a newscast from the year before, and the year before that.

Summoned by a horn after half an hour, Haley donned his flak jacket, scooped his Magnum from the hall table and the briefcase from beneath it, and sidled cautiously out of the front door. The taxi, a battered Land Rover with graffiti-daubed side-armour, was idling in the middle of the road. He took the steps down to the pavement three at a time and swore as he almost somersaulted over a hooded figure kneeling in the lee of the gatepost.

"Beg pardon, squire!" The man hastily deposited his Armalite rifle on the pavement and fumbled within his camouflage jacket, producing a fistful of leaflets. Peeling one from the pack he thrust it at Haley. "Marigold Dairies. Special offers to celebrate us taking over the round."

Haley crouched down and scanned the sheet. The offers were certainly impressive. "You're certain you're taking over?"

"No doubt about it." The man patted the Armalite. "Daisyhill didn't invest enough in new technology – they're ripe for a take-over."

"Okay; put me down for one pint a day, plus two strawberry yoghourts on Saturday."

"You got it, squire."

The man ducked as a bullet clipped the gatepost and whined away. Haley ran to the taxi, suppressing a twinge of conscience; Daisyhill had given conscientious service in the six months since it routed the previous company.

'HELP TO CREATE A CLASSLESS SOCIETY!' exhorted the spray-painted slogan on the side of the Land Rover, 'BUILD A GUILLOTINE'. Haley scrambled into the passenger seat, gasped out his destination and wedged himself expertly as the driver launched the vehicle forward with the grinding crunch that signified a disintegrating clutch plate. At the end of the street two mechanical diggers came into view, surrounded by a mess of soil, torn tarmac and cascading water. One was ripping pipes from beneath the pavement, the other pulverising them with its grab. Haley viewed the scene with irritation but no surprise, recalling that the local water company had recently lost its contract.

"Mobile to the Zega Building." The gaunt-faced driver hung his microphone, flicked unkempt grey hair out of his eyes and chuckled as the diggers fell behind. "Hope you remembered to fill your bath."

"I didn't," Haley said shortly.

It wouldn't have helped much, he reflected. Last time they'd had to rely on bowsers for three months while the new company struggled to overcome the impact of its rival's scorched-earth policy, and the old company sought to discredit the newcomer by distributing leaflets linking it to the typhoid epidemic of '96. When

18 / *Market Forces*

that ploy failed they'd laid mines along the street, taking out three pipelayers, a bulldozer and an innocently bystanding mobile grocery store. It had been a noisy, dirty and exasperating period.

"You work at Zega then?"

"Yes." Rather than await the inevitable, Haley added "I test the vidgames."

"What, before the shops get them?"

"Before they're released, yes."

The driver whistled softly.

"Now there's a job my lad would die for. Started years ago with Sonic the Hedgehog, he did, now he's South-East Region Diamond Joystick Holder, three years running."

"He's done well."

"He works at it. Lives on his console. Me, I preferred football. Old-fashioned, I suppose, but it was more sociable. You got anything new coming that I can tell him about?"

"Not that I can talk about, I'm afraid." Haley said. "You know how it is. The competition's fierce."

The Land Rover had closed on the rear of a scarred red bus. It was labouring heavily and churning out clouds of dark fumes. As Haley studied the peeling poster on the back there came a rising roar that swamped the clatter of the Land Rover's engine, and a shabby blue bus surged past them. A glittering, smoke-trailing splinter flickered through the air and burst on the road, engulfing the outside front wheel of the red bus in a gout of fire. The vehicle swerved wildly, mounted the pavement and embedded itself explosively in the front window of a derelict department store.

A mile along the road the blue bus halted to pick up passengers. Before Haley's driver could manoeuvre round the obstruction, a white jeep with a flashing red light-bar slid past and tucked in front of the bus, blocking its progress. They watched the uniformed occupant climb out, walk over and lean into the cab. A moment later he withdrew and returned to his car, pocketing an envelope. Reversing smoothly, he waved the bus on its way.

"Must be his birthday," Haley remarked ironically.

"It's the pay-cops' motto," said his driver. "Stop one and buy me."

The Zega Building was a steel and crystal monolith soaring upwards from a skein of pedestrian conveyors. Haley stepped nimbly from taxi to conveyor and was borne smoothly into the building's glittering interior. He ignored the bank of lifts, choosing instead the less claustrophobic challenges of the escalator system. Ten minutes later he emerged on Level 53, having despatched a would-be mugger on 28, dodged a plunging suicide on 35 and weaved past the beggars who circulated constantly through the building via the shining steel arteries.

Kimberley, the Research Department's receptionist, was already installed at the front desk. As Haley approached, the PA chimed into life overhead.

"Bomb alert! Please evacuate the building. Bomb alert! Please –"

The announcement was cut short as Kimberley reached under her desk and flicked a concealed and unauthorised switch.

"Hoax call. First one of the day's always a hoax."

Noting his quizzical expression she said, "No mail today, I'm afraid. PostOff's holding it to ransom."

"Again? For Christ sake!"

"They need the money. Their chairman just awarded himself a million pound rise, for the second time this year."

"So are we paying or playing?"

"Playing, this time. We put a snatch squad onto the roof of the sorting office about ten minutes ago. They're working their way down looking for our bags but it could be a slow job; the place is booby-trapped like crazy. We also have a hit squad in their headquarters, stalking their chairman."

"How come? His little extravagances are hardly our business."

"True, they're PostOff's. The shareholders put out a contract on him, so we picked it up to offset the cost of rescuing our mail."

"Smart idea." Haley drifted toward the coffee machine. "Marriot'll be bringing the new vid down. Send him straight through. Oh, and can you fix me another car. Somebody tried to boost mine last night."

"How many did it take with it?"

"Just two, far as I could see."

"Two's fine – every joyrider we waste gets us a reduction on our insurance premium. Fix you another by lunchtime."

Haley wandered through to his office, shrugged off his flak jacket and hung it over his chair. As he settled behind his desk the telephone rang.

"Haley."

20 / *Market Forces*

"This is Tracey from BriTel Surveillance, Mr. Haley," said a husky female voice. "We're currently in a position to offer a tape which would enable you to identify a subordinate who is planning to replace you in your role as Senior Tester."

Haley sighed. "I'd be more excited to find one who wasn't."

He hesitated, pondering. BriTel were reliable but their products never came cheap. And he was certain he already knew the potential usurper; Kaye, of the deferential tone and ingratiating smile. He would rely on his wits to discover the intended manner of his downfall.

"Thanks, but I'll pass."

"If you're quite sure."

"I am, thanks."

Before he could consider the implications further there was a knock on the office door and Marriot strolled in. Zega's Senior Technician was wearing two-foot dreadlocks over a white lab coat over jeans and a T-shirt which bore the legend: 'IF YOU'RE INNOCENT WHY AREN'T YOU IN JAIL?'

"Haley, my man. Today's the day and this here's the one that's gonna red letter it. It's gonna bomb the market and make Zega bigger than Virgin Narcotics."

Haley smiled and took the proffered cassette.

"I seem to have heard that line before."

"Maybe, but then I was lying."

"Supertedium?" Haley read from the label. "What the hell kind of title's that?"

"A working one. Marketing'll come up with something sexier before we launch."

Haley moved towards his console but before he could take his seat the room vibrated to the deafening whup-whup-whup of approaching rotors and a flexible steel ladder clattered against the outside of the window. A moment later the panes burst inwards under the impact of a masked, black-clad figure. As he hit the floor the intruder opened up with a Uzzi machine-pistol, bringing down a section of ceiling. Behind him two more dark figures tumbled in through the smoke and dust now billowing about the room.

The first arrival waved the Uzzi menacingly at Haley and bellowed: "Hand it over – fast!"

Haley gaped at the cassette in his hand, then glanced across at Marriot. Marriot nodded resignedly.

Market Forces / 21

"Let him have it, Haley. You Xintendo clowns got no class – just like your vidgames. You won't get away with this."

"We're scoring quite nicely so far, pal." The leader plucked the cassette from Haley's grasp and tucked it into a pouch on his belt. Then all three figures sprang to the window and scrambled up the ladder. The throb of the engine quickened and the helicopter lifted away and drifted lazily out over the canyons of the city, heading towards the river.

Haley yanked out his Magnum, ran to the window and loosed off a futile volley of shots.

"Don't bother, my man," said Marriot languidly.

"But they're getting away!"

"Only subjectively."

The technician's hand went to his pocket and drew out a small. black cube with a red button set into its crackle-finish surface. Walking to the window he studied the scene, and as the helicopter soared out over the river he thumbed the button. Instantly a dazzle of orange light flared within the helicopter's plexiglass canopy, then the machine blew apart.

They stood together in silence, watching the debris whirl down. As the last fragment splashed into the grey waters and vanished from sight Haley said:

"Very neat; no collateral damage. Bonus points to you. How did you know Xintendo'd try to steal the prototype?"

"BriTel. They bugged a conversation and we bought it. Your boy Kaye helped to set it up I'm afraid. Figured you'd get busted for losing it and he'd take over your desk."

So that was it, Haley thought, remembering his own call. Trust BriTel to try doubling up on its sale.

"This is what they were after." Marriot drew a second cassette from his pocket and handed it reverently to Haley "And believe me, we are talking seriously priceless here."

Haley returned to the console in the corner of the office and swept dust from the controls. Carefully he inserted the cassette into the input slot, donned the Virtureality visor and pressed the button to activate the system.

Instantly the grey-walled office faded and in its place there materialised a small, cluttered room, high-ceilinged and decorated with drab flock wallpaper. Warily Haley surveyed the dim interior, taking in the shabby furniture, the uninspiring watercolour

22 / Market Forces

suspended from the picture rail, the ancient wooden-cased wireless standing on a table in one corner, the budgie cage hanging from a stand in another. He glanced down and was surprised to find himself weaponless and devoid of body armour. Instead he was clad in a shapeless jumper and corduroy trousers that hung over mud-smeared boots. Moving slowly across to the window he stared out. Before him stretched a narrow street of terraced houses; sunlit and silent. There was no traffic in sight or even audible. The whole setting seemed sunk in a warm, noiseless torpor; the only visible movement came from the far pavement where two youngsters crouched in the dust, playing marbles.

With infinite caution Haley worked his way through the house, alert for any of the myriad traps he had encountered over the years, straining to detect any other presence. There was none. He padded softly to the back door, eased it open and peered out at the tiny lawn with its flanking flowerbeds, its bird-table and its adjacent vegetable patch. A hoe was leaning against the fence and he armed himself with it and stood waiting.

Nothing happened. Nothing moved, other than a pair of bright butterflies and a sparrow that paused to drink at the bird-table then flew on. After a while Haley reached out with the hoe and prodded experimentally at the vegetable patch, prising a clump of weeds from the soil. He prodded again, lazily, and again . . . Gradually the pile of weeds grew. Presently his solitary pottering was interrupted by the arrival of an amiable brown dog at the garden gate. He let it in, petted it and led it through to the kitchen where its bowl was waiting. While the dog ate noisily Haley made a pot of tea, then settled in his armchair with his cup and the biscuit barrel. Later he tidied the kitchen, then cleaned out the budgie cage and afterwards returned to the garden and began trimming the lawn with a pair of shears he found in the tiny potting shed. Towards the end of the afternoon he wandered back into the house, made himself another pot of tea and switched on the wireless, catching the distinctive opening of the Billy Cotton Band Show . . .

"Wakey wakeyyyy!"

Haley jerked back to reality and stared round the office, dazed and disoriented. His eyes settled on Marriot. The Technician was clutching the cassette and the visor and grinning broadly.

"Sorry about that, man, but four hours is plenty."

"Four hours!" Haley dragged his wrist up and gaped at his watch.

Market Forces / 23

"But . . . nothing happened! In fact nothing happened slowly! No booby-traps. No opponents. No competition. Christ, there was so much nothing it was hypnotic." He took the cassette from Marriot's fingers and peered at it, as if its secret could be deciphered that way. "What is it? What the hell theme is it based on?"

"A British Sunday, circa 1950," declared Marriot. "And it's gonna take the market by storm."

Haley stared at him, and even before the PA chimed out its latest bomb alert he knew the prediction was correct. Already he felt a growing urge to re-insert the cassette and slip back into the programme; to submerge himself in sunlit tranquillity and pat the dog and start on the bedding plants, and afterwards stroll in safety to the local pub and enjoy a pint, unhurriedly and without the need to keep his hand near his sidearm . . . As Marriot chattered enthusiastically at his back Haley continued to gape at the cassette; stunned, unable to rise. Supertedium . . . It was new and brilliant and dangerously addictive. It was the ultimate in escapism.

Adrian Wilson

Quite a Night, Darling

At first she thought the lights were just the sun flooding her rear-view mirror as the car levelled with the horizon. The shock of realisation only came with the third or maybe fourth flash as they inched to her bumper and pulled back, allowing her a glimpse of the blue roof-bar. Fast lane passengers gesticulated or just opened their mouths at her – passing goldfish behind glass.

She was dry. There was a hair or small bone at the back of her throat. For the last hour she'd been rolling her tongue fruitlessly over at it.

The hangover lingered, along with the nursery rhyme refrain of a pop song she'd stabbed from the radio five minutes ago which looped remorselessly. She took out her handkerchief and blew, hoping to dislodge both irritations.

The crawling container-wagons had noticed now, and were clearing a space for her. She pulled through and onto the hard shoulder.

No thoughts would come in the minute she spent cocooned, waiting for the tap on the glass, only that her mistake had probably been in crossing the county line, nothing more. Here there were no cities of any consequence, no drug rings or baseball bat gangs to keep them busy – the devil finding work for idle hands. She was a distraction from numb patrol.

It was true what they said: he looked young enough to be her son. There were recently cropped and weeping acne scabs around his neck.

"In a bit of a hurry aren't we?" he smirked.

He asked about the car, was it hers, a sleek cap prodding the front tyre for emphasis.

She couldn't reply. The hair or bone was swelling – a pony's tail; dinosaur limb.

"Are you okay, lovey?" he asked, his tone a mixture of condescension and suspicion. "I think you should be aware this car is in a dangerous condition.

"This you see . . . " he ran a finger along the rusty jagged edge at the bottom of the door, " . . . could give somebody a nasty gash. Same goes for the back bumper."

The bodywork. That was all. She wanted to cry. Why were they bothering her with it now?

"Filler," she managed to blurt, which only seemed to make him more suspicious.

"Have you been drinking?" he asked.

She saw the bottle rolling empty, tensed and shook her head like an obstinate child. She couldn't take it, booze. Never had been able to.

"I think I can smell alcohol."

"It's nine. Just."

The blockage in her throat was only allowing little scraps to tumble out. She thought of the way a balloon squeezed in a fist would escape in miniature between the fingers. She sounded like a half-wit.

"Do you have your documents then?"

He folded his arms and winked back at the patrol car as she eased herself back behind the wheel.

The dash compartment was crammed. Petrol chits and empty cigarette packets. Dwarf spanners and wheel nuts, clanging as she fumbled.

He shuffled the licence and forms with impatience.

"You're not John Read."

"No."

"I thought you said this was your car?"

"Named."

"Wait here."

She watched the uniformed back disappear into the sun, epaulettes glinting at the shoulders. When the policeman re-emerged from it his stride seemed to be invested with new purpose.

Whatever was in her throat wouldn't let her swallow and the pop song's pummelling creased her brow.

"I'm sure I can smell alcohol on you," he said proudly, "so we're going to breathalyse. Follow me please."

Her legs wouldn't take her that far. She glanced down at the tarmac and saw its patina of rain shimmer. Her knees were liquid, ankles like a pair of drunken librarians balancing towers of teetering books. Crossing the line, her only mistake.

In the back seat of their car she was overcome by the need to curl up and go to sleep. She caught the end of a sentence from the front and started, wondering if she had actually dozed off for a second or two.

She looked at the neck of the driver. Flaps of skin over a starched collar. She imagined them continuing down the man's body, like the rings of a tree. A fold for every year on the force.

"Jesus you're not kidding," the neck said to the windscreen, "like a brewery."

The other man handed her a contraption. It looked, she thought, like an organ freshly torn from a robot.

"You blow into that bit. Take a deep breath first."

She put the white pipe to her lips and puffed her cheeks out, letting the air escape through her nose. Breathe like a trumpeter. Fill the stomach and hold it there. Feeling dizzy she passed it back to him.

"You haven't done it properly, darling," he pronounced with strained patience, "try again."

If she fluffed, they'd want her blood. She did it again, making no effort to deceive.

He smiled like an encouraging father this time, as he took the machine back.

She sat, looking for signals of activity, aware of the need to make herself seem human. Say something.

"Bit party," she managed finally.

"Must have been quite a night, love," the neck replied miserably.

Quite a night. It had started like many others, with that unacknowledged thunder in the room. Knife and fork on the plate like fingernails breaking along a brick wall, cup threatening to shatter in the saucer. And the TV.

"Well, Mrs. Read, you're not over the limit anyway."

"Wha . . . "

"The reading shows there's alcohol in your system but it's below the line."

The TV had been the source, the root of that thunder, but she'd never realised it before. She'd asked him to fix it too many times. So she'd opened up his tool box.

"Do I just go?"

They were trying to trick her somehow.

"Get that car fixed, that's what you do, darling. Pronto."

"I'd get home and sleep it off if I were you," the neck added, stabbing vaguely in the direction of consideration.

She was a gymnast at the bottom of the rings. Superhuman effort required. Her hands tried to grip metal, shoulder against the padding. A massed choir and orchestra were pounding out the pop song's refrain now, the subtle flattening or sharpening of a few choice notes had turned it into something quite stirring, but at the same time cautionary.

Something would happen. She needed to throw up. She'd fall, a guilty spreadeagle. The car would splutter and die. Somehow they'd realise their mistake.

Back behind the wheel she let the bile up into her mouth, sour-metallic. The bone or hair, or whatever it was, shifted momentarily then wedged itself back in place. And her legs. Over-ripe fruits; feet flopping across the pedals.

No turning back now, even though crossing the border had been a mistake. Stunted trees and ashen fields here. The police car sped past and she took the next turn-off.

The quarry was cut from a dip with whiskery brambles on its sandy face. The pond was dank and reed-cluttered.

She parked at the brown water's edge and wound the window down.

She tried to remember the first time they'd chanced on the spot – on the way to the coast it must have been – unwrapping sandwiches from tin foil on the baking bonnet, him poking in the murk with a stick, skimming flints through patches of green moss.

She saw the empty bottle rolling, the contents of the toolbox scattered – the hammer with the contoured redwood handle and the hacksaw's sky blue set of teeth. She never could handle it, the booze, and she'd asked him to do something about the TV. She remembered stepping gingerly down the gravel drive, later, for the green sacks from the shed.

Secured at its top with strimmer cable now, the first one plopped into the clay as, with a grunt, she hauled it from the boot.

Richard J. Hand

Landlord and Lodger

"I'm sick of it!"

"Eh?"I exclaimed, with no time to speak.

"All this D-Day doo-dah." With this, Mr. Beech beckoned me into his front room. He was seventy-eight years old, and the room was heavy with the past. Nothing new here, apart from a postcard on the mantelpiece which I'd sent him from my Easter holiday. "Sit down," he gestured. He picked up the remote control and eyed it suspiciously as though it were Exhibit A. Having found the correct button, he stretched his arm full length and pressed it like a detonator. He wouldn't have been surprised if the television had exploded. Neither would I.

"Just look at it." There were the sharp young troops and the fading old soldiers. The dignitaries too. The Queen stood under an umbrella. "Look. The poor old Queen stuck in the pissing rain in an old mac." He jutted out his jaw and shook his head solemnly. I kept quiet. I wasn't sure if he was going to say more about the position of today's monarchy. "All this *fuss*. Bloody D-Day."

"Wasn't it important?"

"'Course it were, don't be daft. But it's all these ceremonies. It were more than all that, or *different*, anyroad. This ain't the way to remember it. Perhaps we shouldn't anymore. Different world now. Fifty years gone by . . . it's a long time . . . Time to let it go. Forget it." He looked thoughtful. A question occurred to me.

"Were you there, Mr. Beech?"

"Aye. I were there." He muted the TV.

On a table in the corner of the room was a picture of him in uniform. Smiling. Not much older than me, but he looked it. Why? The brilliantined hair? The fading black and white? That was then, this is now? Maybe it was just me resisting and refusing to believe.

"I'll tell you what I remember about D-Day. It were the night before we were going to invade. We were all nervous. I were on patrol. I reached some bushes and trees. I stood stock still, quaking in me boots. I gripped me gun. It were too quiet, all too quiet. Suddenly, I heard a rustle in the bushes, a movement. I raised me gun and shone me torch where the noise were coming from. It were one of our squaddies havin' a shit. As long as I live I'll never forget the look of utter bliss on his face."

"You should be on television with that one!"

Landlord and Lodger / 29

"Aye, if only, lad, if only." Mr. Beech really did have the most incredible collection of anecdotes, but for now he steered us back to the present: "How are things upstairs?"

"Oh fine, fine. But actually I've got some news." My heart was in my mouth. He looked at me curiously. "Aye, I could tell you were skulking about, lad." I took a deep breath as quietly as I could. "Well, um, I've decided to move out at the end of the summer."

"Oh." Mr. Beech looked very surprised. "So, you're giving in your notice?"

"Yes." Mr. Beech paused for a moment's reflection, and then he sparked up.

"Oh well, lad! I've enjoyed having you around the house. It's been over a year now, hasn't it? Flown by. You were always a good lodger, you paid the rent on time and it were always legal tender! You were never too noisy either." My music was usually drowned out by the volume of his TV set. "So what are you up to? Are you leaving Hull?"

"No – I'm keeping hold of the job I've got at the moment. But I'm considering moving to another city before too long. I may even go abroad." Mr. Beech chortled. "Um, I'm moving in with a colleague at work. She's paying a lot on her mortgage so it'd help her out."

"Oh, it's a young lady is it?" Mr. Beech winked suggestively and rubbed his palms together.

"No, nothing like that!"

"Ooh, that's a shame ain't it! Mind you, you never brought many ladies back here – not to my knowledge, anyroad. Perhaps you smuggled them in when I weren't looking! I'm no prude . ., but if I'd caught one of them I'd have got her doing the housework!" As he said this he had got out of his armchair and popped over to his cabinet. He slid the door open and produced a wine bottle. He took a corkscrew and removed the cork with a mouth-watering "pop". He filled two glasses almost to the brim. I glanced at the TV. The pageant of remembrance continued in silence.

"A special treat for you: a parting gift. Some of me home-brew!" I took a sip.

"Mm, this is lovely cider!" I exclaimed, ingratiatingly.

"It's wine." I hate it when I do that. So do all my family and friends.

"Oh. Ah. Mm."

"Chateau Beech." For a moment we savoured the taste. Mr. Beech looked at me. "Aye, you've been a good lad. Shame to see you go – never mind, never mind." There was another silence. I couldn't break it. Mr. Beech snapped us out of it:

"It were wash day for me today. As you know, I've got a lady who helps me out. She does me shirts and linen, but I never let her have a go at me underwear, especially not with all the problems I've had *down under*." He winked slowly and solemnly. "So I gave me pants a right good boiling on the hob this morning. I bet you're glad I gave you a glass of me wine and not a bowl of soup, eh!" He thundered with wheezy laughter. I shuddered involuntarily. When he calmed down he told me with some authority, "I'm a respectable retired gentleman who keeps a couple of lodgers in me house. But I don't owe anyone owt, so I can be a dirty old bugger if I want. It's great being able to get away with anything. A great life." He didn't want to debate this, so he changed the conversation swiftly:

"Are you having a summer holiday, lad?" I never had chance to answer this question. He levered himself out of his armchair and picked up the postcard I'd sent him from Dublin at Easter. He held it at arm's length in the stillness of thought. "Mm," he said "it's a grand city is Dublin."

"Oh, you've been there?"

"Aye, aye. Don't think I've sat in Hull all me life! I've travelled, and not just in uniform either."

"You didn't tell me you'd been there!"

"We'd have been here all year if I started telling you all my tales! Right, Dublin. When I were there I went to have a look at the house Oscar Wilde were born in. Yes, I'm quite a cultured chap really! I used to read a lot, y'know, when I were a lad. Not anymore. I haven't read a book in years." His eyes fixed on the flickering colours of the TV screen for a moment. "Anyroad, where was I? Oscar Wilde. Well, when I were there they made such a fuss about this son of the city of Dublin, how proud they are of this genius and all that gumpf. But I kept thinking it weren't always that way: they weren't always so proud of him. And do y'know why? 'Cause of the way he were inclined . . . he weren't a 'lady's man', you understand . . . And the hypocrisy of it makes me sick."

"Yeah – you're right. And I'll tell you something else . . ." he leaned towards me conspiratorially and whispered gruffly, "*There are more bum-boys in Dublin than in the whole of England put together.*" I have mastered a response to these sort of statements. I give a toothy smile and emit a kind of half-laugh, half-sigh; but I always say nothing and resist nodding or shaking my head. But I'm sure Mr. Beech would not have cared what I thought anyway.

Mr. Beech had already finished his wine, and before he filled up his glass to the brim again he held the bottle and waited for me to take a good gulp of what I had left. I could tell he was wondering how could I enjoy his home-brew with the silly little sips I was taking. Gulp. There you go, Mr. Beech. Glug, glug, glug: full glass. Afternoon drinking has always been my undoing. It ensures that I'm fit for nothing in the evening. Sometimes I'm even hungover before bed-time. Mr. Beech's wine on the drizzly afternoon was certainly taking effect. I'm a pleasant drunk: I tend to be overcome with tingling sensations of hilarity mixed with optimism. As I sat there, I decided that the place wasn't so bad after all. The walls in my room were damp: the wallpaper had wrinkled and curled off the wall and was so discoloured by mould that even Roderick Usher would've called in the decorators. But I never complained to Mr. Beech: the same indisposition had afflicted his walls and ceilings. No, I'm happy here. I smirked. But no, it *is* time to move on. Then came the kind of comment I dread:

"You know, lad, you remind me of myself when I were young." No, don't say it please, don't say it. I'm not you, and I won't be. I really do not know what upset me so much, but in an instant I wanted to escape to my room and pack. Yes, that is the word, *escape.*

"Look, I'll tell you a story. There is something that haunts me, something from way before the War and all that stuff. The 1930s were hard times, very hard times. And I dare say that we in Hull had it as bad as anywhere. I were lucky: I didn't know any different, and like the naïve fool I was I thought it would all get better. It did, in time – not mentioning the War, eh? – but what about all the people left by the wayside? I were young, *younger than you.* I knew a very poor couple who lived just up the end of the road. The house is full of students now. Blaring music and vomit on the pavement on Sunday mornings. The filthy bastards. Anyroad, the couple were skint. The old man had got cancer, couldn't work anymore. His wife set up his bed by the parlour window, he could hardly get up the stairs, you see. I used to go round while his wife

32 / *Landlord and Lodger*

to keep the old boy company. He were so weak and hungry he kept saying he wanted to kill hisself. Slit his throat with his razor. We used real razor blades in them days, you really could've done yerself in. Not that me old friend could've: he were too weak to even shave himself. His wife did it for him. The rest of the time she kept the blade out of his reach, like you would with a baby about the house. When I were there he kept saying, 'I want to die' and I kept telling him that it'd get better, and that his weakness of body were a sign that he mustn't do it. Naïve bloody fool that I was. He must have been right sick of me! One morning I went round to see him. The front door were locked which were unusual. In them days we hardly ever locked our doors. I went into the backyard and looked into the kitchen window. The old boy had put his head in the over. He were still alive, I could tell. I put me hand on the door, and then I turned sideways, ready to force the door open with me shoulder. But I turned me back and left. His wife came round our house later, in a terrible state. She'd got back home at four, and her old man were dead, of course. She asked me if I'd gone round that morning. I were quaking in me boots, I felt as though *I'd* killed him. 'No, no' I said, 'Well, I did go round in the morning, but the door were locked so I came back home.' I'll never forget the stare she gave me. She looked long and hard. 'Didn't you wonder why it were locked, lad?' I remember feeling sick and scared. 'No, no . . . I thought he'd gone out with you . . .' She gave me a look – how can I describe it to you – she gave me a look as though I'd told her the Humber had dried up overnight. But she didn't say owt else, she just turned and she looked so broken. She knew I knew: but that wouldn't have brought her man back to her. I'll never forget that. And I've never worked out what I should've done. There's no right answer, it changes from day to day. And even now – sixty years later – I still don't know. I'm no philosopher, but I suppose life's like that: it should be clear-cut and dried like all that crap on the telly, but it never is, and we're fools expecting it to be so."

He looked at me as if I could give him an answer. I stared back at him, impassive. A few moments passed like that, and I saw his eyes change from being hounded to being genuinely scared. What could I say? What face did he want to see? What should I have done with my expression? Then he turned his head to the television, his lips thin and bitter. "What answers could I expect to get from him?" he thought, or so I'm sure he thought. Did he want me to

Landlord and Lodger / 33

finally condemn him or redeem him all these years after he let a man die? Was he even trying to blackmail me ("Don't go, lad!")? But above all the other enigmas that filled those moments in my landlord's front room was the simple question: why did that story remind him of me? Did he see before him, slouched in an armchair and holding a glass of home-brewed wine, the naïve young man who abounded with hope? Or was I already the born-again cynic that turned away?

*

I left a few weeks later, but that one afternoon with my old landlord sums up the year I lived with him. On the day I left, I remember packing my bags and cardboard boxes taken from the supermarket. The room, which had never really been mine, had become Zen once more and echoed. It was a sunny day and I looked out of the window at the kids in the street and mothers with toddlers in buggies. I'd seen them most days over the last year and seen them age so slowly that none of them had seemed to age at all. Even the babies who had learnt to walk. Here were people and their houses – homes – people "belonging". And here, for a moment, was I, pissed off at being so rootless. I wanted to belong, although I was shocked to see that even the home-bound, the settled in place and the established in age face doubt, face dilemma and irresolution. It was a sunny day, but most of the year it seemed to have rained, with an occasional day of fog for light relief. For a long time I watched the street and I remembered being a child watching the rain against the window, tapping and dripping down. Touching the glass: it was cold. At home, a place I lost long before this. Once more, in Mr. Beech's house, where he'd lived nearly all his life, I was ready for departure. The thrill of escape, the thrill of tomorrow . . . You know, I think I once really did believe that I could meet everyone in the world. I believed in the future. But now I know that the past is everything, because the present is too fleeting to be held and the future is just useless speculation. We draw on the past to define what we are now, and to make sense of other people too. In Mr. Beech's home he'd shown me his collection. Boxed-up anecdotes in dust or wrapped in the newspaper of their time. He even found a place for me in one tale. I will collect and hoard such stories too, but before I start I must understand that the point and the meaning of all of them will never be fixed.

Johanna Fawkes

Et in Arcadia Ego

My mother tells me Sinclair is dead. She heard from someone in the pub.

"How, when?"

"Four or five weeks ago it seems. I don't know more."

Her words crawl up the phone line. I look out at the darkening fields. I know what happened in South Africa today. I don't know what became of my friend a month, maybe more, ago. The news travels slowly through me, like a bruise.

"I'm surprised Cathy hasn't been in touch," my mother continues into my silence.

"It must be fifteen years since I left the agency. She'll have enough on her plate." I hope the years will insulate me.

"You were more than colleagues, darling." My mother knows they won't.

I watch my face focus in the window as the daylight dims. The person who knew Sinclair is on the other side of the glass.

Sinclair gave me my first job in advertising. He liked my voice on the phone, as I cold-called my way round agencies. My hard won degree proved worthless without a Sight & Sound certificate. I refused to learn to type, certain it would condemn me to secretarial eternity.

He swims towards me now, an air bubble loosened from the sea bed, as I saw him then: leaning back in his swivel chair, slight pale frame encased in heavy chalk-stripe suit – with waistcoat – wing collar, bow tie, highly polished lace ups resting on the desk.

He can't have been more than twenty eight, though he seemed from another century.

Bloody Hell, I thought, it's Lord Snooty.

"Enter, enter," he instructed, swinging his feet to the ground and rising to shake my hand.

"Coffee?"

"God, yes," I replied, not yet schooled in the ways of interviews, "I've got a terrible hangover."

That was it, really. A few perfunctory questions established I could neither type nor take dictation and the job was mine.

We adjourned to The Sea Dog, opposite the Jermyn Street offices. The whiskered landlord had relocated the pub from the Haymarket to the Azores. Marine memories covered the dark wooden walls and his thick, bared arms.

"George takes his role seriously," commented Sinclair, as the drinks arrived. "Never set foot on a boat, but acquired all the nautical accoutrements on appointment."

"Is this a hint? You want me to apply Stanislawsky to advertising?"

"Au contraire. Our job is to play the part, not believe in it." A manicured hand, stiff white cuffs and gold links, pushed wayward strands of limp blonde hair away from his small, pale eyes.

He said he would teach me enough about the business to get a better job – and he did. But first I had to learn the office rituals. Many of these involved running personal errands – popping across Piccadilly for Fribourg and Treyer cigarettes, collecting collars and cuffs from Jeeves, the Drycleaners, or handmade shirts from Turnbull & Asser. He insisted on the very best. If it wasn't By Royal Appointment . . .

Wardrobe and props, an assemblage of labels and insignia. I couldn't imagine him in jeans, though he once said he was a Mothers of Invention fan. Did Sinclair get trapped in his own uniform?

Each day began with imperious demands for coffee. Bristling with resentment, I plonked the china cups on his paper-strewn desk, hoping some would spill. Until I decided to offer coffee at regular intervals, making it my gift, not my job.

Sinclair finished *The Times* Crossword by about ten thirty, and then it was on with his fine wool cape and 'off to the bank'. Well, they did cash his cheques. My morning job was to lie. The ponderous MD, Mr. Edwards, who'd set up the company just after the war, and made sure it stayed safely second-rate, would lumber in at intervals, gaze at Sinclair's empty chair and turn to me.

"He's popped out to the printers, meeting someone from *The Times*, a lunch in Fleet Street . . ." I didn't care whether he believed me.

After all, I was coming to work – late – from different directions most mornings, on the back of bikes, in cabs, or just by Tube. When I finally arrived, it took me a day to type a letter. I never remembered to enclose whatever was supposed to go in envelopes. We had to protect each other.

Once Sinclair left, I spread out the day's papers, scanning them for items relevant to any of our clients. It was a slow process, waiting for the nervous print to settle, the pages scraping and crackling as they turned. Coffee didn't so much calm as synchronise the shaking. By mid-morning I'd digested the lumpy memory of the night before, the blurred anonymous struggle on the bedsit floor.

At lunch, I joined Sinclair in the extension:

"Welcome to the Canis Mare, dear girl. What will it be?"

"I'll have one of your medicinal lagers, please."

"Landlord, two more Pils here."

"Did your doctor really say it was good for diabetes?"

"Near enough, near enough. And your medical emergency?"

"Low alcohol level," I laughed, drinking the lager quickly. "Maintained intake till three am, but there's been a marked decline in consumption since."

"Soon put that right."

I scrabble through my desk looking for mementoes, proof that he existed. I find a post card, an engraving of a castle ruin near Montrose, his point of origin. He was on holiday, visiting old haunts. He spoke often of his childhood home, his love of the countryside he grew up in. His massive italic script fills the space: 'Et in Arcadia Ego.'

But I have other images of his past, a dark and cold house, with only his ancient mother for company. Perhaps he was forbidden to be a child.

He signs himself Umbra, his translation of Sin Clair.

Another card, a Matisse, after I remembered his birthday: 'Gracious Lucia, I thank you for commemorating my senescence.' I bought him Paul Foot tracts, he bombarded me with Bernard Levin and Peter Simple. When we got on very well, this was reversed. I still remember the date. I know this man's birthday. I carry his history, real and imagined, in mine. Why has no one been in touch?

High Tory and low Socialist, we introduced each other to favourite haunts, with trepidation and pride, like kids from opposing gangs revealing their hideaways.

Sinclair belonged on Jermyn Street, with its ancient crafts: cheese-makers and herbal perfumeries, all the double barrelled shop fronts, barely converted to decimal coinage.

It was 1977. Piccadilly Circus – only yards away – was full of green hair and safety pins. We kept to streets whose only contemporary reference was bunting for the Queen's Silver Jubilee.

He escorted me, walking on the outside naturally, down Jermyn Street, explaining the charms of Paxton's and Floris, pointing out Trumpers, his barber. If he was ever conscious of my market stall outfits, their nasty fabrics, sagging seams and stuck zips, he never said.

Terry, a colleague from Sinclair's days with the Westminster Press, sometimes joined us in Jules bar or Rowley's restaurant. Terry was a bore, in my opinion. Drunk on a couple of glasses of house red, he slurred and leered at me, while rehashing tedious news stories from the Sixties with Sinclair.

"Remember the Ronan Point scam?"

"Terry helped ID the dodgy cement," Sinclair explained to me. "Didn't you, old man?"

"Biggest housing story in decades. Made all the nationals. Now look at me, scuffling the streets with egg on my tie. It's a bloody shame."

"Damn right, my friend." Sinclair filled our glasses again. "You should apply to my Grant for Greatness Fund."

"What's that then, old boy?"

"My idea for preserving monuments such as our good selves for the nation. Does it not seem improper that the petty minded of this world should hold such sway, while we free spirits and sybarites are condemned to a life of pensions and annual increments? It is the very Death of the Soul, is it not?" Terry and I nodded enthusiastically, and finished the bottle.

"Then we must create a Fund, to reward those whose contribution to humanity cannot be measured in mere pounds, shillings and pence. They must not be allowed to wither on the vine. They are our heritage, and should be nurtured from the collective purse."

"This is positively socialist, Sinclair," I warned him, giggling.

"Anarchist, surely, oh lady of lightness. You Reds believe in labour not art."

I decided to trust his fondness for Zappa more than the fob watch and take him into Soho, my landed inheritance. As my mother's daughter, I was welcomed into the many clubs she frequented: downstairs dives which shared entrances with banks or cinemas, unknown to the latter's clientele; smoky rooms above restaurants or in council estates; all the splendid secrets of afternoon drinking.

38 / *Et in Arcadia Ego*

I loved this hidden squalor. So did Sinclair, though his aristocratic demeanour seemed out of place amid the stumbling artists and scruffy drunks.

My mother, one of Soho's grandes dames, was the arbiter of his status here.

"He's very stylish," she pronounced, one afternoon when Sinclair had picked his way carefully to the toilet, his head delicately balanced on his shoulders, like someone carrying water from the well.

"Or pretentious?"

"No, I think he's a character in his own story, a jewel of his own design."

My mother rings again the next morning. The day is brilliant and winter sharp. But Sinclair's death has sent me to bed with old movies.

"I've found Sinclair's address. I thought you'd want to write to Cathy."

"Do you remember how grand he was?"

"Of course I do, Lucy. That splendid flamboyance. And fondness."

"Yes."

There's a pause. My throat is full. What have I left behind?

"I'm sure Cathy would like to hear from you, sweetheart."

Cathy, his small, dark wife, occasionally joined us for a drink after work. Sinclair and I would become louder as we swapped unsuitable ideas for press launches:

"A hovercraft down the Thames . . ."

"With Edwards water-skiing behind . . ."

"Trailing cerise balloons with the brand name in purple . . ."

"In a matching lurex outfit . . ."

Cathy sipped her vodka in silence. Our badinage petered out and they left. I trawled the West End for a fuck.

"A man likes to protect his woman," he explained the next morning, as we nursed our respective hangovers. "To know that she is vulnerable, that she relies on him."

"Even if he has to demoralise her into submission, eh?" I muttered irritably.

Sinclair stared at me sternly for a moment, before rising for his first appointment across the road.

At the time, bewildered by concepts like marriage and fidelity, I assumed she was another of his idiosyncrasies, like hand-made shoes. Now I see she was his anchor.

One day, Mr. Edwards came in and, instead of asking about Sinclair, moved behind me, as if inspecting the press cuttings. He placed one hand on each breast, for just a moment, then walked out, both of us speechless.

"The man's a perv, a dirty old bastard, can't you stop him?" I asked Sinclair, when he returned several hours later.

"Don't really see how, old girl, don't really see how." And he disappeared again.

I suppose the situation was too perilous for him to risk a confrontation. Edwards was increasingly impatient and I was often ordered out of the pub to hold fort. Sinclair rarely returned before four. Terry was dying and Sinclair spent an hour each day at the Middlesex Hospital, refusing to explain his absence.

"I'm getting calls from Golden Grip, and Butter Dew aren't too happy," Edwards announced gravely, late one afternoon, just as Sinclair slumped into his seat. "I don't pretend to understand media relations," he said, making a little huffy noise to signal humour. I kept my back to him, studiously retyping an overdue letter. Sinclair bared his teeth slightly. "But they want more column inches."

"Brickbats and Bouquets", Sinclair said, airily. He had no intention of enlightening Edwards on media mystique.

"Yesterday, bouquets, today, brickbats. Tomorrow, who can say?"

Did Edwards realise his Head of Media was almost comatose? Probably not. Sinclair's grandiosity simply expanded with alcohol, the hand performing ever larger, ever vaguer arabesques. He never faltered in words or action, though the soundtrack slowed noticeably. Edwards probably put this down to diabetes, Sinclair's faithful alibi.

Unlike him, I was beginning to stagger, my body betraying me at last. I had been so proud of my capacity. Now it took effort to straighten my knees, fix an elbow on the bar. I needed things to hold on to. When a client asked if I was drunk, I stopped making phone calls.

Sinclair disappeared for two days after Edwards' visitation. I invented urgent appointments, out of town profiles, local radio interviews . . .

On his return, Sinclair retrieved an Olympic portable from under the desk and raised an eyebrow to signal black coffee. I propped a shortbread in the saucer, hoping to restore his blood sugar levels.

"What's up?" I asked.

"Wait and see," he replied, whistling. At intervals, he leaned back in the swivel chair, hands locked behind his neck, or called for more coffee. By opening time, he'd come up with a campaign for three clients. Over the following weeks they made the Nine O'clock News, Nationwide, LBC and all the national press.

"Sinclair's Lesson Number One: he who can control his genius with finesse and judgement, must be showered with bouquets. Then the bastards will leave him – or, gracious lady, her – alone." Edwards didn't come near us for months.

I find a 1977 diary under the cards. August 16, Got Pissed; August 20, legless. Bank Holiday, Great Weekend – I think.

Each week, I acquired new accessories – black eyes, a broken arm. My face was red and puffy, there were cigarette burns on my skirts. My tights were laddered, my knees scabby as a schoolgirl's from falling in the street. I didn't care; I was invisible.

When I came in with bloodstained shirt cuffs, Sinclair became alarmed:

"You don't think you should cut down a soupçon?"

"Cut down what?" Hands on hips. Yes, Sinclair? I just can't wait to hear what you have to say on this subject.

He brushed his fringe back, adjusted his cufflinks:

"Nothing, never mind."

"Hmh."

"Care for a coffee?"

I wrote to Cathy today. Just to say now important he was. How much he taught me. And protected me – he must have saved my job. I asked her to let me know what happened. Why didn't I know how much his death would hurt? I could have invited him to my fortieth (he could have invited me to his).

Sinclair was appalled when I stopped drinking.

"Good God girl, you weren't that bad."

"I was. You don't know the half . . ."

Et in Arcadia Ego / 41

"But it's so bloody . . . ignominious!" Abstinence offended him aesthetically.

"And you're in a worse state now . . ." Sinclair continued, when I arrived, as so often, hours late for work.

"But I can't sleep . . . I lie awake till dawn, then . . ."

"That's all very well, but we've got a business to run."

I floundered through the papers, baffled by the machinations of the outside world. My failure to detect my addiction, in the face of overwhelming evidence, disqualified me from holding opinions.

My confusion was sartorial, also. I arrived as someone else each morning. Vamp in fishnets one day, twin sets the next, like an amnesiac prompting recall. Hippy or punk, girl next door or TV presenter? Wardrobe changes speaking of desperation, not disguise. They lacked Sinclair's panache.

Moments kept evaporating: I'd go out for a sandwich and come back two hours later. The mistakes, omissions and commissions, which had been so forgivable when hungover or pissed were now criminal offences. I was sentenced to typing labels for months.

A couple of months later, I suggested my mother and I treat Sinclair to a birthday lunch. I was trying to show what a brick I could be on bitter lemon.

"You're no fun any more," my mother complained. "We used to have such a good time together." She took another gulp – it was a food-free lunch, of course – and turned her out of focus features in my direction. "Promise me darling, just promise me, you'll have a little bitty whisky at my funeral . . ."

"Ask not for whom the Bells toll, eh?" I replied.

Sinclair guffawed.

"But it must be said, my dear," he intoned sorrowfully, "that you are not the exuberant effervescent Lucia of times past."

"I'm not throwing up in the street either," I protested. "You never saw what happened after. I could have died, you know . . ."

"Come, come," they tutted in unison. Sinclair picked up the wine bottle and began to pour. I placed a hand over my glass, the first self-protective gesture of my adult life.

Sinclair sulked at my sobriety. I had deprived him of a playmate. My excuses for his absences got thinner. I wasn't trying any more. I'd survived the Titanic by swimming to the shore; he didn't think he was wet.

A note from Cathy arrived today:

> Sinclair wasted away after he lost his job. I daresay
> the booze didn't help, but he said he'd rather die than
> give up. He spoke fondly of you and of your times
> together at Edwards' agency and I am sure would be
> pleased at your current success. He was bitter that
> his own talents were unrecognised. He died of despair,
> really. It took years.
> Yours, Cathy.

I last saw him a few years ago, in Jermyn Street. He was wearing
the same clothes, but had shrunk inside them.

"How goes it?" he asked.

"Good, good. I'm doing OK. You?"

"Flotsam and jetsam, you know, flotsam and jetsam. Advertising's
a cold hearted business now." He shoved the greying hair out of his
eyes. "Still on the wagon?"

Yes, I smiled. He shrugged, and we parted.

Stuart Allison

The Gate

"Winter's out," said Joe.

Greening hedgerows slipped slowly by, filling his view from the passenger seat.

George considered the budding twigs, the damp verdant verges. "Ay. Mebbie," he agreed.

It was as much as the men had said all that afternoon. More than on some. Silence between them was understood, accepted, welcomed even. Their response to a shared situation; their imposed solitude. This silence held no hidden meanings for them. It was companionable and voluntary. And, like their habit of equality, it marked their mutual dependence.

George turned the ancient Land Rover off the black surface of the lane and slowed to avoid the potholes and ridges that formed the farm track. The suspension was no longer able to reduce these shocks of the rural and he was sensitive to the older man's painful limbs. He had no wish to aggravate joints already inflamed. Concentrating on the road immediately before him, George missed what Joe could hardly avoid as they approached the house.

The car parked in front of the dilapidated farmhouse was shiny and new. Seemed fresh from the show room.

"Representatives," muttered Joe, cynically.

Looking up, George was arrested by the bright gleam of red. He grinned at the sheen, incongruous against the dun, weather-warn bricks. "Fool's errand," he predicted.

Joe relaxed again, confident George would keep the salesman waiting until they had seen the cows in from the field across the road, and milked. Afterwards he would tell the lad · they were all so young these days – they wanted nowt. No sale. And the flash youngster would go, disconsolate. And George would get supper ready by the normal time whilst Joe saw the chickens gathered into the hen house for the night.

George allowed the bumper of the battered old Land Rover to kiss the smooth red plastic of the saloon. Gentle as a cow's tongue at its calf.

As they were getting out, the stranger approached through the side gate, mud and muck clinging to the suede of his shoes.

"Townie!" Joe's tone was contemptuous, and loud enough to reach the young man's ears.

But George said nowt. He halted in his tracks and stared at the newcomer in silent disbelief.

Smart, confident, the young man ignored Joe and stepped eagerly up to the farmer.

"Michael!" George welcomed the young man. Took him in a warm embrace that expressed deep affection.

"Hiya, Dad," the young man said.

He glanced at Joe and only nodded.

Alone, Joe finished the milking. He patted Betsy on the hocks, urging her from the stall and recalling the day when he and George had spent four hours rescuing her as she lay stranded on her back in a ditch. They had saved her new born calf that day, as well.

George, his favourite briar trailing fragrant smoke and signalling an end to his day's labour, trod too carefully into the cow shed. He looked at the soft eyed cows and avoided Joe's stare.

"Haven't seen Michael for years. Ten years. Mebbie more." George was well aware that Joe knew this. "He'll likely be stoppin'. For a while."

Joe nodded. He refused to return George's unfamiliar parting smile.

Alone, he hushed and heyed the slow cows from the shed. They wandered unguided along the track and spilled onto the lane until Joe urged them into the field opposite with calls of encouragement and much arm waving.

The gate was bad still. George, had he been there, would have lifted it, closed it with one hand. Joe's rheumatic limbs hauled it heavily over cloying, hoof-churned mud until it was a few feet from the post. From there it was more a question of stopping it from swinging back open before it was secured. The loop of faded baling twine, once bright orange nylon, was split and threatening to give again. Joe tied yet another knot until it looked as if it might hold the barrier shut for one more night.

In the kitchen the food smells were unfamiliar. Joe looked forward to the fry-up that always followed their visit to the market. But the lad had the stove, his back to Joe, talking to George.

Joe took a step from the worn doormat.

"Boots off, Joe."

He raised eyes and eyebrows at the unfamiliar demand and saw the familiar face coloured with embarrassment. He crouched uncomfortably and worked at the string, covered in cow muck, that formed the laces.

"Michael, say 'hello' to Joe, son. You've known him long enough."

The outstretched hand was clean, manicured, but open enough. Joe stood, free of one of the boots, and wiped his hand on the seat of his green corduroys before he clasped the other. Both tested the strength of grip, Joe's, in spite of age and rheumatism, the stronger. Michael washed his hands before returning to the food.

"Used to bounce you on me lap when you was a lad," Joe recalled for all of them, bending with difficulty to his other boot.

George nodded his fond memories.

"Used to," Michael reminded them.

"Michael's fetched his own 'erbs and things to meck us a fine supper, Joe."

Joe nodded and tried not to let his disappointment show.

For ten years they had eaten together in silence. Never a need for words. With Michael, George was all talk. Joe half listened. His other half sought something. Finally he knew it was simply the customary silence of companionship he was seeking.

Neither father nor son made mention of letters never written. Each understood the other would not write. And the farm had managed to remain unconnected to the world by wires. Michael lived a hundred miles and more away with wife and child and work.

Until the previous day.

"And now?"

"Divorce is absolute now, Dad. I stayed with her till then. Promised her I would She's got Carol so she'd best have the house as well. It never had a hold on me anyway. I'm free now No ties."

"Stay with us as long as you like, Michael. The place'll be yours when I'm gone anyroad. Might as well get used to it."

"I disappointed you by going out of agriculture, Dad. I know I did. It's not too late. I can learn."

"Not that easy. For a townie." Joe gave voice to the thoughts George's love would not allow him to express.

"Give the lad a chance, Joe. He were born to the land. Likely he'll pick it up quick enough."

Father and son talked into the night. Through hours George and Joe had shared at chess and brag and gin. Their shared words droned into Joe until the sound of his exclusion drove him to his early bed

46 / The Gate

with little more than a mumble. They barely paused to acknowledge or reply.

Later, out of pitch black, and through siling rain, a knock came unfamiliar at the front door. Local callers, friends, used the back door. A stranger, drenched and savage, cursed the cows that had him off the road and almost in the ditch. George nodded an apology and smiled the driver off. He yelled at Joe to help him get the herd back into the field.

Michael lit the gateway with the static car but refused the comfort of its dry interior. He bore the soaking with the men as they hushed and shushed and herded the cows from the lane and back through the open gateway. To Joe's surprise and George's admiration, Michael played a useful part.

"You should've made the gate secure, Joe. The times I've told you."

Joe allowed the unjust rebuke to pass in silence. He said nothing of the untold times he had badgered George to fix the gate.

Michael fiddled with the broken twine to no avail. "This should've been fixed ages ago."

The look of accusation he shot at Joe, under the harsh glare of the headlights, did not go unnoticed by his father.

George walked the track to the cow shed and found a better piece of twine. The gate was fast secured to the leaning post.

Dawn, damp with early mist, saw Joe milking the morning cows alone for the first time since he had nursed George through a fever seven years before.

In the kitchen, eggs that George invariably fried were scrambled healthily by Michael. Seasoned not with salt and pepper but with dried herbs from his own collection. Joe declined the speckled pale concoction and broke three fresh eggs into aromatic fat. Ate them with thickly buttered slabs of crusty white bread to soak the golden yolk, the clear beef dripping, from the plate.

"Scrambled eggs contain less cholesterol, you know, Joe."

George nodded, his son's up to the minute knowledge wanting his agreement, and watched Joe's feast with envy well hidden. "What's so wrong with Michael's cooking you're forced to do your own?"

"Piss pale mush! You know how I like my eggs." He stabbed one harshly, pointing at the yellow, bleeding, dripping from the bread. "Like that. The way you do them."

"He's stoppin', so you'd best get used to it."

"Ay. So it seems."

Michael, sensitive more to his exclusion than to the tension, tried to intervene. "It's not important, Dad. I've no wish to impose my own ideas on either of . . ."

"Impose is right." And Joe stalked out into the growing sunshine to make good the repair on the gate before he said too much.

"Teck no notice, Michael. It's just the change. He feels threatened, I reckon. Give 'im time and 'e'll get used to you as a man. He were fond enough on you as a lad. He's bound to come to terms with you in time."

"Is he? It's my experience that men who don't like change are generally stubborn and narrow minded. Bigots. It might be worth considering how efficient he is. Does he make a contribution worth having?"

"Joe's experienced, lad. He's utterly dependable, you know . . ."

"Really, Dad? That'll be why we were chasing cattle in the pouring rain at midnight, then."

George wanted him to know that the gate was his responsibility, that Joe had tried to get him to repair it. But this proud young man admired him and the father welcomed the respect of the son. Joe was broad backed enough to take a little blame. It would do no harm.

"Just one of those things, Michael. Could've happened to anyone. It's not important."

"And if the driver of the car had been killed?"

"Look, Michael, me and Joe have worked this place together for most of our lives We've done it on our own ever since you left and your mother . . . passed away. I'd be lost without him."

"Will the farm support three of us?"

"It supported your mother and you for long enough. It supported a family."

"I'm talking personal income, Dad. Not pocket money and housekeeping."

Michael really wanted him to choose from what he saw as the alternatives. But he had no wish to put these into words for his father. He had sacrificed his home and left behind his family in the expectation of finding something new and lasting on the farm. Now

48 / *The Gate*

it was beginning to look as if he would be left with nothing but the car, his few personal belongings still in his suitcases and a bit of personal capital. Little enough to show for the years of marriage.

"There are no wages here, Michael. Never were. We each have what we need. The rest goes back into the land."

"Subsistence farming, Dad? I always imagined the place was a little gold mine."

"Never was. Never will be, Michael. Land's too poor. I'm sorry, lad."

Michael knew enough to recognise the truth. It was truth, after all, that had ended the marriage after his undiscovered affair. He trusted his father. Understood there was no subterfuge in what he had told him.

The father saw the son's dilemma. Realised the gulf between their respective needs and dreams and hopes was unbridgeable. Gave his lad the means to leave.

"When will you move on, son?"

"It's not just the money, Dad. It's . . . well, I need something a little more . . . , you know?"

"Up to you, Michael. There's room enough. There's food. A bed. And work. Always plenty of work."

"No. I don't think so. Not for me."

"Ay. Mebbie."

There seemed no reason for him to prolong his stay. He was intruding, and there was nothing for him on the farm. He might as well be on his way, wherever that might be.

"No time like the present, eh?"

"So they say."

Joe came back up the track. He had fixed the gate with timber borrowed from the hay loft, a bolt found in the workshop. The barrier was secure and firm. The herd would stray no more.

The red car approached him, slowing as it did so. Michael wound down the window. "I never intended to cause any ill-feeling between Dad and you, Joe."

Joe nodded and touched his cap. He turned as he followed the car out of sight.

In the kitchen George was wiping tears from his eyes.

"You and your bloody eggs!"

Joe nodded. Put the kettle on.

"You can cook your own damn breakfast in future, Joe."

Joe pondered. Wondered if the change was permanent.

"Gate's fixed."

George scowled at him, recalling how he had let Joe take the blame. It would be hard to forgive him the reason for the lie.

"About bloody time."

Joe nodded and poured water on the tea in the pot.

"Touch of spring about this mornin'," he said as he recalled the feel of the soft morning air, hoping things might now return to normal.

But George just stared at him in hostile silence and Joe recognised that things would never be quite the same again.

Ian Smith

Jereminsky's Oranges

"You've got to be ready for most anything out here. How do you think I've lasted all these years?"

These are the first words I hear, when I've struggled through the door to get into the Club and regained my balance after skidding wildly, through puddles spreading across the verandah floor. The rain's driving hard against the wall and pouring in miniature torrents through the mosquito gauze. As I'd guessed, Jereminsky's standing behind the Bar, declaiming with vodka in hand.

I'm new to the District and to Africa, so I've to take it on trust that this *is* the worst rainy season anyone – which means Jereminsky – can remember. Normally there's rain regularly from November to April, but never a deluge like this for weeks on end – with earth and sky merged in a single wetness of grey.

Though we'd never admit it, we envy Jerry and the other farmers for a variety of reasons. Now especially. The non-stop downpour is holding up the work which counts for most – touring the District to implement the Development Plan.

Touring in the rainy season means miles of cycling through the wet, trying not to fall off when the path vanishes under water, or squelching along in boots made soggy from wading innumerable *dambos* and streams. The long dank day ends behind mosquito-net defences with the whining squadrons already probing for a single perfidious tear, whose treachery will yield a feast of blood. And when the lamp is extinguished, for sleep in blankets more drenched and odorous than yesterday, the long-assaulted canvas overhead succumbs to storming rain, swelling the dripping influx into a cold cascade.

But, even these conditions can't spoil the satisfaction of getting the job done. Far better, still, than endlessly revising plans while rain drums down on roofs of office buildings, making it impossible to hear oneself speak. The frustration at being unable to travel more than a few miles out of the township can easily be imagined. Floodwaters have turned the *mopane* forest beyond the farms into a swamp, sweeping culverts and bridges away and severing roads in every direction; gulleys have eroded into small chasms, destroying village gardens; several people have been killed by lightning. There'll be no end of catching up to do, when the floods subside.

It's not surprising that the Local Authority employees, whose contribution is vital to success, are losing interest. Their priority will be to get into the gardens to attend to damage as soon as the rain slows down.

"You ought to be farmers," Jerry smirks, well aware of our feelings. "We can always do something worthwhile. There's equipment to repair – buildings to improve. Would anyone like to give me a hand?"

"No, but you can buy us a beer!"

Willard comes in soon after me and wisely stamps the mud off his feet onto the coconut matting in the doorway, before venturing through to the Bar. He's Headteacher at the Secondary School. Our local hero. Was educated there himself. Smiling condescendingly at me, he uses his handkerchief to wipe away the streams of rainwater running down his face.

"You didn't believe in our customs, did you? Old Shimunenga's fixed things with a vengeance. At least, when it's over, most of our people will have good crops."

"Well, I'm not going with you again, that's for sure. There's been enough rain for years already. I'd never have believed it would begin even before we got home."

It was far more serious than my answer suggested. I'd been deeply and permanently impressed, in spite of the coincidence it must surely have been. The sudden lightning in a clear sky and the unbelievably quick arrival of the storm had, in some way, stretched my beliefs, given me a changed consciousness – as if being at the ceremony had given me a new perspective on God – of how he might be perceived in relation to natural powers. It suddenly became easier to understand why the people of Kamala won't take the timely repetition of nature's cycles for granted.

For most of Willard's people – after four years of near drought, poor harvests and losses of livestock – the outcome will be a profoundly happy one. And it must be satisfying, having a *muzhimu* – demi-god, to whom you can relate. They believe Shimunenga and the other *mizhimu* came down from a spirit heaven and will take you to see traces of their arrival, the unmistakable and impressive imprints on rocks by the river, not far from the township.

"*Bakaseluka*," the people say, meaning both that the demi-gods came down and that they're partially reincarnated in the tribal Chiefs. So it's understandable that Shimunenga should continue to help them, fitting comfortably into their way of life – someone with whom behaviour and beliefs are directly negotiable. This is a more credible arrangement than they can find in the alternative religion most of them profess to adhere to, and which is mediated by an alien priesthood. It seems more natural to put one's trust in a being who directly demonstrates his potency and his charisma.

Wealth is counted in cattle, and all their beasts are paraded each year for Shimunenga, in the certainty that he's looking down on the devoted display. Later, in the sultry heat of October – the suicide month – when clouds are lowering in the sky and distant objects are confused in mirage-like shimmering, everyone goes to pray. They gather, where Willard took me, in an ancient grove, thick with the scent of violet blossoms of the *mafumafma* tree and ask for Shimunenga's help.

Jereminsky's moved away from the Bar, drink in hand, to where I'm standing, next to Willard, and makes as if he's going to put in a comment – perhaps even to jeer – begins to say something, thinks better of it and goes back to where he was.

Willard is fortunate that his teaching is not much affected by the floods. Nearly all his pupils are boarders, staying at the school unless they have relatives in the township. So his work goes on normally, except that he shares in the general reprieve over incoming paperwork. No mail's got through for three weeks now. To be honest, we're happy without the official stuff; when it arrives, most of it will be out of date and can be safely ignored. Such is the nature of Civil Service matters.

Perhaps because he's jealous of our long leaves and pensions, Jereminsky takes every opportunity of deriding Government regulations, twisting meanings in the letters he writes to us, while professing to seek clarification. But the ending is always monotonously the same:

You are sir,
my obedient servant.

He's in this vein today, having saved-up another story at the expense of the Civil Service.

"Just before the last bad rains," Jereminsky says, "there was a difficult rabies epidemic. It was hard on the Veterinary Officer who came to organise the tie-up and inoculation of animals which might have been in contact. He'd a king-size problem – or two of them, you could say. The Game Ranger was on transfer to the

Jereminsky's Oranges / 53

Luwungu Valley and was taking his pets with him, Big Fellow and Little Fellow. Your Rabies Ordinance says all animals in transit have to be inoculated, since they can't be observed long enough for it to be pretty certain they're not infected.

"Civil Servants are so tied down by bloody regulations," he went on – taunting us, "young Richard had to inject them. His teeth were chattering, but he did it."

You'll appreciate the Veterinary Officer's devotion to duty better when I tell you that even the smaller of the Game Ranger's duo was a fully grown lion. This was a story we hadn't heard before. Jerry rarely told the same one twice, except when putting newcomers in the picture about himself. But this time he'd overdone it – in the light of what was to happen later.

After a pause, to allow his tale to be appreciated, Jereminsky keeps the initiative by shouting out at me,

"Hey man, what's happening about the bloody supplies? There's only enough booze here for another month or so!"

"It'll be fine," I announce, in the immediate questioning silence, trying to sound more certain than I feel. Any other answer would have produced an outcry. With no sign of a let-up in the rains, many essentials are getting short and the District Commissioner has asked for a relief boat. Everyone has handed in lists of needs, with the Dispensary taking priority. I radioed these out yesterday and heard from Provincial Headquarters that Noel (instantly nicknamed Noah) Jones had been nominated to bring them. He'll come by river, but will have a devil of a job getting through the Kavubu Flats, where the normal channel is obscured by floods several miles wide.

It's revealing what people regard as indispensable for their survival. Predictably, Jereminsky only needs his favourite vodka.

Now Jerry's finally got tired of propping up the Bar and has come to sit with me. No one forgets the first time this happens. It's an initiation beginning with an unnerving ritual performed by his little finger, which was reset badly after being broken, so it can't bend. Having plonked his glass down on the arm of his Morris chair, he sets the finger into action vigorously, to fix the drink exactly to his liking. Using a vertical jabbing motion, the finger stabs down repeatedly, submerging and smashing his slices of lime and crashing the ice noisily up and down and around the glass. Not

54 / *Jereminsky's Oranges*

a drop is spilt.

"An old Polish habit, to improve the taste," he says, but his explanation doesn't fit, since his present addiction is to the latest fashion for vodka and tonic.

The next part begins with Jereminsky asking rather fiercely, "Do you mind if I smoke?," which leads to unimaginable suffering. His pipe is stuffed with a mixture of sun-cured Burley, grown on his farm, and wild native tobacco. The little finger making a further masterly contribution. The resulting flare-up is villainous and awful. Long before the pipe is burning to Jereminsky's satisfaction and blue-grey coils of smoke are spread implacably around him, there's evidence of its mephitic effect. Humans sheer off and insects flee, as soon as he produces his pouch.

After this prelude, which seems to have a mollifying effect on him, he begins his saga in gentler style.

"I never used to smoke, you know," he'll say. "We learnt to do without when we came North. My father didn't smoke once when we'd crossed the Zambezi. It was too easily detected at night. But we put up with worse hardships, to get away from those bloody burghers and find decent land. In the end we succeeded. Six families started out; only two made it here. Several times when we thought we'd got it right, the *tsetse* fly came in or the water supply packed up, so we had to move on. The only folk who gave a damn for us or offered help were the missionaries.

"We had to struggle for a living. You could tell when someone had made it. It was the time they'd put corrugated iron on the roof to replace the thatch. That great day came for me when I sold my first good crop of flue-cured tobacco."

This was when Jereminsky rebuilt his farmhouse, in burnt brick, and, a few years later, transformed his *stoep* into a fine, pillared portico, like something out of the American deep South.

I'd sit there sometimes to talk with him, like a visitor to a timeless island, surrounded by a sea of wild African bush, where waves of white bougainvillea billowed over encircling walls and poinsettia flamed around the best lawn for hundreds of miles. His wife had Jereminsky bring in blue-white water lilies from the river for the pond, perhaps re-awakening memories of a more gracious life before she came out to marry him, and she introduced gentler and more aromatic shrubs to counteract the vehemence of the other, more vibrant foliage. She died of blackwater fever long ago, and he,

Jereminsky's Oranges / 55

heartbroken, planted the long drive of blue gums, in her memory. Nowadays it heads out elegantly, past the purple-blue haze of the jacarandah trees to his precious acres of oranges.

One evening, in the midst of all this fecundity, I asked Jereminsky if he'd ever been to the grove. He half-avoided my eyes and seemed shamefaced, for the only time I can remember. There was a lengthy pause.

"Yes, I went there once, long ago," he said.

"What happened?"

"It began to rain the next day."

Then, most unusually for him, when confronted with a subject he knew about, he began to talk abut something else and I had the feeling his years in Kamala had changed him a lot.

It was his pride about the oranges that led to the event I'm going to describe. In fact it happened while I was away on leave but the old-timer neighbour he'd invited to inspect his crop told me about it on my return.

Jereminsky was showing him round when a *pi-dog* suddenly lunged through the orange trees and bit the visitor on the leg. There was no doubt it had rabies. It came on with that ghastly lurching run, and the bite in the visitor's calf bore ominous traces of hydrophobic saliva. Because the Dispensary was out of vaccine, the only way to save the man's life was to get him to Hospital at the Line of Rail, fast. So Jereminsky and neighbour dashed out from the orange trees, jumped into Jereminsky's car and tore off in a cloud of dust.

As he drove Jereminsky was cursing the farmer's lot generally, with so much to guard against, that avoidance of risk was impossible. There seemed to be little else he could do to make survival and success more certain. Worse than that, he was now on a mission to save his neighbour and was afraid things could get worse. He'd heard humans could spread hydrophobia. Suddenly he had a thought about how to reduce the odds. His visitor was obviously in poor shape or he'd have managed to keep out of the way of that damned dog. So perhaps . . . ?

"Do you go to the dentist often?" says Jereminsky.

"Not any more," says the neighbour.

Jereminsky's hopes begin to rise.

"Why's that?"

"Oh, I got so many bad teeth, I had to have 'em all out. I've got false teeth now."

"Fine," says Jereminsky, hugely relieved and putting the brakes smartly on. "Give 'em to me or I won't take you any further!"

So the visitor takes out his false teeth and Jereminsky puts them carefully into his pocket, delighted he's improved his chances of being around to produce the next year's crop of what ought to be his most magnificent oranges. But it was not to be.

I arrived back from leave the day after Jereminsky died. We buried him next to his wife in the little cemetery at the back of the *Boma*. Both local missionaries came. Neither of them knew which religion he was. He'd have been pleased by their initiative. They worked out some kind of ecumenical farewell and we put him to rest under the *oranjeboom* tree, which was just beginning to flower.

Shortly afterwards it began to rain.

Grace Harvey

Dead Man's Shoes

I had reached the decision that Bollinger had to die three weeks ago; it was just finding a foolproof way of doing it that had created the delay. Now everything was ready. Within the hour he would join me, and the trap would be sprung. I settled down in my hammock, content to enjoy the respite while I waited for the man to appear. The canopy of trees dappled with light and shade, created a welcome cover from the sun, as my mind drifted back.

I had come to the island on instructions from head office, who wanted someone on site to oversee the work in progress. There was also the little matter of a scandal, but that is another story. The island off the coast of Queensland opened up a new world for me and within days, its beauty seemed to cast a spell.

Those first few weeks I had explored as much of the island as I could, absorbing the atmosphere and the placid, easy going nature of the inhabitants. All around me, the intense colours of the plant life, the warm sun, and the deep blue of the sea, made this a tropical paradise. The islanders themselves did not have the typical broad flat face of the aborigine. The men were tall handsome looking individuals, the women very beautiful, but extremely shy.

It was on the tenth day that I found her. I was traversing a rather rocky part of the island when I heard the sound, obviously a cry of pain, and I hurried to locate the source. Rounding a shelf of rock I came upon her lying on her side, one leg twisted under her, eyes appealing for help. I gently picked her up in my arms and thinking quickly, decided to take her back to the bungalow and resolve what to do with her once I had assessed the injury.

The injury was merely a sprain. What was intriguing, however, was that on enquiry no one seemed to know where she had come from, and her inability to communicate with me made the problem even more complicated. In those first weeks, she seemed to be overcome with shyness and apprehension, which disappeared once she was on her feet. She would gaze at me with adoration, seeming to know exactly what I was thinking. I tried to tell her that she should go back to her home, but the sadness in her face put me off taking any action.

Soon, I was completely under her spell. I would gaze at her, totally bewitched by her beauty. Her long dark hair, the smell of her warm body close to mine, and the coquettish way she looked at

58 / *Dead Mans Shoes*

me, would have turned any man's head. When I told her she could stay, her joy showed clearly in those dark liquid eyes.

I began to look forward to her company on returning from work in the evenings, her gentle acceptance of my needs serving to tie us closer together. Now and again I made a half-hearted attempt to find out where she had come from, glad when these enquiries came to nought.

Four months later, the mystery was solved. Bollinger, a planter, who lived in a remote part of the island came to claim her. When she saw him she ran towards him, a light shining in her eyes. She obviously adored this man.

"How do you do," he said, in a voice that belied the rough cast of his features. "I'm Ian Bollinger. I've been at my wits end searching for Maya. They told me down at the dock that she was with you. Many thanks for looking after her, old man."

"I'm Mark Travers," I said, shaking his hand.

"Sorry to have put you to any trouble," said Bollinger, "but I'm here now to relieve you of the responsibility."

I looked at this big coarse man, then at Maya, the incongruity of the situation rendering me almost speechless. Glaring at him, I said as cuttingly as I could, "I suggest we let her make up her own mind about that, don't you?"

It was obvious, however, that Maya had already done so. Now that Bollinger was here she had eyes for no one but him. Thinking quickly, I invited the man to stay the night before returning home. Perhaps, if she had time to see us together, she would come to her senses.

During the evening, Bollinger told me that an accident a few years ago had affected her vocal chords, robbing her of the ability to make any but the most basic of sounds, although her ability to understand was perfectly normal.

Lying awake, long into the night, I thought about the disaster of the evening just past. Maya had not looked at me once, quite content to snuggle up to that repulsive man. It was obvious that she would go away with him in the morning. Knowing that I could never let her go, I needed to persuade Bollinger to stay around for a while, but how? I was still trying to come up with an answer the following morning when Bollinger solved it for me.

"I say, old chap, how about putting us up for a couple of weeks while I get some supplies together? Being in the bush for so long,

I've forgotten what civilisation is like."

"Stay as long as you like," I said, trying to hide my satisfaction. "There's plenty of room, and I will enjoy the company."

Bollinger turned out to be just as coarse as I had at first thought, as well as being a scrounger. He settled into the bungalow as if he owned it, and what was worse, Maya seemed unable to comprehend the true nature of the man. She still followed wherever he went, totally ignoring me. I had to admit that he treated her well, his normally loud voice softening whenever he spoke to her.

After two months I could barely be civil to the man. It was at this time that I made the decision. As Bollinger would not willingly give her up, I would somehow have to get rid of him. Racking my brains as to how this might be achieved, a plan slowly formed in my mind. I knew that it would require exact timing, and for now I must ensure that Bollinger was so comfortable that he would have no urge to leave.

In my walks across the island, I had come across a dense area of jungle. It had fascinated me at the time because it was so far off the beaten track. I remembered sitting there quietly, enjoying the scenery, only the brightly coloured birds disturbing my solitude.

The spot wasn't as peaceful, however, as I had first thought. After sitting there, enjoying the beauty of the place, I decided to have lunch. Having brought with me a raw steak and a bottle of wine, it was my intention to light a fire and cook the steak. I had just removed the meat from its container when suddenly in the undergrowth behind me, I heard the rustling of dry leaves, and jumping up quickly upset the tin, the meat spilling onto the ground. From the bushes emerged a huge snake, slithering along in search of prey. Ignoring me, it moved to the place I had vacated, and swallowed the steak whole. It then continued across the open space, finally disappearing into the bushes on the far side. I got out of there as fast as I could and had never been back since.

Later, the natives told me that I was lucky to have come out of there alive, as that area was known as a haunt for the native taipan, a snake known to achieve a length of nine feet, whose bite was twenty times more powerful than that of a cobra, and contained enough venom to produce paralysis and death within a few minutes. Dropping the meat onto the ground had been fortuitous, as the taipan had been guided to it by its sense of smell.

I had found the perfect answer to my problem. Two days later, I

60 / *Dead Mans Shoes*

rose and left the house at my normal time. Retrieving the knapsack I had secreted in the long grass outside the bungalow, I made my way towards the area I had visited on that other occasion. I was now aware that the snake could appear without warning, and therefore I tried to avoid the areas of dense undergrowth as much as possible. In this fashion, I eventually reached the clearing.

My plan was simply to find out how long it would take the taipan to realise that there was food available. Removing the lid of the container I had brought with me which held an enormous piece of raw meat, I quickly tipped it out onto the ground and replaced the lid. Retreating to a safe distance, I then waited.

Within three minutes of placing the meat, I heard the familiar sound of the snake, slithering through the trees to one side of me Moving as quietly as possible, I immediately put as much distance as I possibly could between myself and the area that the sounds were coming from.

The sight of the taipan was even more frightening this time because I was now aware of just how dangerous it was. However, it did not appear to see me, but moved to the other side of the clearing, towards the meat. Opening its mouth it swallowed the meat whole, and within seconds, again disappeared into the jungle.

I was jubilant, sure that my plan could not fail as long as I could lure Bollinger to this spot. However, this was where my plan fell apart. I could think of nothing that would persuade him to enter the jungle, and therefore resolved to engage him in conversation that evening, in the hope that something would arise that would bring my plan to fruition. Before leaving, I searched for a short heavy piece of wood, hiding it at the side of the clearing.

That evening, I invited Bollinger to join me on the verandah. He was rather taken aback by my request as I had previously made it obvious that I preferred my own company. However he agreed, and over a bottle of whisky, we started to talk. He told me he had been on the island for fifteen years, and had never entertained thoughts of returning to England. In the course of the conversation, he mentioned that his hobby was collecting orchids. This seemed rather a strange hobby for a man with such rough manners, but apparently he was extremely serious about it.

Suddenly realising that this was the very opportunity I had been searching for, I quickly informed him that I knew of a place that was teeming with the things. The upshot was, we arranged to set out at seven the next morning, spending the best part of the day searching for orchids. He had at first wanted to bring Maya with him, but I managed to persuade him that the jungle was not the place for her.

My reverie was suddenly interrupted by the sound of someone whistling, and within seconds, Bollinger came through the door. He looked more than ever bedraggled and unkempt. It was obvious that he had slept in his clothes, his body odour telling me that he had not even attempted to wash before emerging.

"Are you ready?" he bawled at me. It was never his habit to talk in a quiet way, confirming my feelings of superiority towards him.

"Right," I said, "just have to get some provisions so we don't starve, and a bottle to wash everything down."

This obviously suited Bollinger. As long as someone else provided the sustenance, he was quite happy to partake. We were ready by a quarter past seven, hoping to be away from the open country before the sun became to hot. It was soon obvious that he was used to the rough terrain, and we moved along at a good pace.

Shortly before noon, we reached the spot. Placing our packs in the centre of the clearing, I looked around for Bollinger. He was standing at the far side of the clearing. I was fearful that the taipan had appeared too soon and my plan would be thwarted, but what he was staring at were a highly coloured group of orchids, the slight breeze rippling their petals. Rushing over to the spot, he knelt down in a gesture almost of reverence.

"Do you know how long I've been looking for this particular species?" he said. "More than ten years. This is the most amazing sight I have ever seen."

I knew it was now or never. He was so distracted by the plants that he was unaware of me creeping up behind him. Kneeling there, he presented the perfect angle and I raised the wood that I had retrieved from the bushes, bringing it down hard enough to lay him out. Slowly he toppled forward, crushing the orchids as he fell.

I worked quickly. Opening my pack I took out the container of meat. This time I had brought offal, aware that the much stronger smell could not fail to attract the snake. Lifting it up in my hands, I proceeded to smear it over the recumbent form in front of me.

When this was done, I put the tin containing the meat back into my pack. Quickly I moved away from Bollinger, and crouching in the grass at the far side of the clearing, I settled down to wait.

62 / *Dead Mans Shoes*

I had just begun to worry that Bollinger would come to before the taipan arrived, when I heard the soft rustle in the bushes that had heralded its previous arrival. Within seconds it was in view, seeming even larger than before, with its brown ridged back and its bright yellow underbelly set off by a rather small head. The head rose up as if smelling the air, then dropping, the snake moved across the clearing. I started up in terror! It was moving not toward Bollinger, but toward me.

Frozen to the spot, I couldn't understand why it was coming my way. True, I was nearer to it than Bollinger was, but the smell of the meat should have been the stronger attraction. I clasped my hands in despair as it came toward me, suddenly realising by this action that my hands were wet and sticky. Looking down, I found that my hands and jacket front were covered in blood. In my rush to smear it on to Bollinger, I hadn't noticed the effect that the dripping blood had on myself.

The taipan was now only feet away from me. I screamed and tried to back away, only to find impenetrable jungle behind me. The taipan lifted its head, its devil's eyes looking at me as it pulled its head back to strike. The next minute I felt a fearful bite in the neck as the snake whipped its head forward. Falling to the ground in horror, I knew that just one bite would seal my fate.

Suddenly, there was an almighty clamour from the left. Bollinger, who must have been brought back to consciousness by my scream, was banging the ground with the same club that I had used on him, at the same time, stamping feet. The taipan raised its head, feeling the vibrations through the ground, then dropping low, it slithered off into the underbrush. I lay back on the ground, aware that for me, it was too late.

Emerging out of the dark whirling vortex I had been assigned to, my head resting on something soft, I was aware of movement beside me. Starting up in terror I felt, rather than saw, firm hands pressing me back to the ground.

"Easy," said Bollinger. "You're too weak to move at the moment, lie there for a while. You're lucky I never travel without my antiserum, or you would be dead meat by now."

Turning my head to look at him, his eyes showed awareness of what I had attempted, but they also showed puzzlement.

"Why?" he said. "What have I ever done to you?"

"You were going to take Maya away," I replied simply.

Dead Mans Shoes / 63

Bollinger's look of puzzlement turned to incredulity. He shook his head and getting to his feet moved away. I watched him wander to the other side of the clearing. Then, obviously coming to a decision, he came back.

"I think you will be strong enough to return now with my help. In any case, I don't think we should hang around here, it may come back.

The journey was a nightmare. Drifting in and out of consciousness, I was grateful for Bollinger's strength. He didn't speak, but now and again, he would look over at me and shake his head as if still puzzled. Eventually, we reached home where Bollinger put me to bed. Seeing that I was afraid to be left alone, he assured me that the worst was over and I must rest.

Early the next morning, I awoke to find him at my bedside. Maya was with him, looking at me with obvious sorrow at my ill treatment of her friend. Bollinger sat down.

"We will be leaving today," he said. "I think you are strong enough now." While he talked, he placed his arm gently around Maya. He looked as if he might say more, but then got to his feet and lumbered toward the door. At the door he paused and as if he could not help himself, burst out, "I know Maya is beautiful! But how could you even consider killing another human being for the sake of a dog?"

With that, dog and master left the room and the door gently closed.

Stephen G. Holden

When Harriet Returns

How long is it since she left? Three hours? Four? Is it so meaningless to try to judge her disappointment by the length of time she has been away?

I take a seat by the flowering cherry. Before me a length of green garden hose snakes out across the newly mown lawn. Each border is colourful and decorous, the black soil neatly hoed. There are the gardening things still to be tidied away, but I think I shall rest just for a while. I have been keeping busy until Harriet returns.

It's so peaceful here that it upsets me. Hard to believe that out there the world is just as hectic as ever, and that all manner of exciting events are occurring while I am sidelined.

There's nothing I can do about that. You see I dare not leave here even if I wanted to. Pack animals would surround me before I got much beyond the gate. The Special Branch people seem to have managed to keep them out of the grounds though. Thank heavens for privilege. I really don't feel that I could bear any more "exposure" at the moment. I feel fully exposed. Bleached photochromically white. I suppose, more correctly to pursue the metaphor, I should say fogged black, like camera film, a negative. Yes that's exactly it. Exposed accidentally to too much bright light and permanently blackened. That's me.

Long white clouds are sculling peacefully across the sky, and bees drone in the lilac. I watch a single bluetit return to the nestbox I once erected for its family. Really I ought to move from here. It does one no mortal good to sit and ponder overlong.

Such introspection, I have found, is merely an indulgence and seldom provides any relief. Better to get on with things. That's how I have conducted my life anyway, getting on with things, being the "action" man. I hold it to be true that it is possible to study an issue far too closely, in which case the whole damn thing can slip out of focus. I have witnessed this happen from time to time in certain of my colleagues to such a degree that they become harnessed by their indecision. Sometimes, I tell them, it is necessary to operate on gut instinct, make a move. Action usually narrows the options, allows one to concentrate one's fire.

Essentially, that is how Sarah and I became involved. I certainly couldn't say it was love that drew me towards her, nor lust even. Not in the beginning. When she made her feelings towards me explicitly known, she became part of my "in-tray" as it were. A small problem for me to sort out before I could get on with other more important things. Before long I chose to return her advances, and we became lovers. It was as simple as and as amoral as that. It didn't seem to strike me as wrong at the time. I don't often suffer guilt.

Our relationship was tasteful, never sordid, and sex with her was rather enjoyable, although I should imagine the satisfaction I gave her was minimal. To make up for that, I suspect that there must have been a certain sense of achievement to be derived from obtaining a close association with a Minister of State. Certainly something kept her interest up throughout the two years we were "romantically involved" with one another.

Such affairs never seem to be quite as secret as one would like. I am almost certain that on occasions during that period, I detected the odd few words of innuendo from my colleagues, which of course I chose to submit to, rather than draw further attention by any show of concern. In retrospect, it's quite amazing that those who knew, or thought they knew, kept "mum" as long as they did. The people in my office appear to have been quite touchingly loyal. On the other hand, perhaps no-one cared enough to even gossip.

It's getting rather cool. Perhaps I'll have to go indoors soon. I must move all those garden tools first, though, they make the place look so untidy. It's most unlike me to leave them lying about. Why I didn't put them away before I sat down here I'll never know.

I suppose it did come as quite a surprise to me when things went wrong. Our relationship had sailed on for so long causing hardly a ripple, then all at once, without warning, the boat was sunk. A most unnerving experience.

You may possibly think that I have been irresponsible in the pursuance of my infidelity, but I can assure you that it is not the case. I have always taken the utmost care that we should never be seen together out of our shared working environment. In my defence, I can only say that my guard must have been down after the conference in Harrogate. I was in fact feeling rather tired. We had found a quiet restaurant. The others had left and we appeared to be quite alone for the first time that week, sharing a drink. I must have felt the need to be close to someone. We were petting like lovesick teenagers when the flash went off. It was something of a shock. Sarah sank her head in her hands in shame. She knew what it all meant. I blustered a lot. Can't for the life of me remember exactly what I said. I think I must have been trying to conduct a damage limitation operation. The two of us being alone together I could easily have gotten away with, a last nightcap after a long working day, that sort of thing. But not the kiss. In general, I find it best not to admit too readily to one's blunders, but this time I really don't have any choice. Attempting to explain myself was a big mistake and I realised it almost immediately. What I should have done was rip the bloody camera from his hands and smash it on the floor, then the only evidence would have been hearsay. But I didn't. What a fool I have been.

I hope Harriet returns soon. I do despise myself for what I have done to her. I must confess I am a little surprised at the way she has let this thing affect her though. She always seemed to have so much spirit. One of the reasons I married the old girl. It's not like her to go off the rails, even for something like this. I suspect she'd been drinking rather heavily. She was in a terrible state when she left, you know. Shouldn't be driving like that.

Downing Street knew before the story became public, summoned me concerning "an urgent personal matter". I didn't need to wonder what it might be. The P.M. offered me a brandy. Then he explained, quite casually I thought, what would be expected of me should events take an "unacceptable course". I knew then that he wouldn't be prepared to back me. Whatever else he had to say was all quite superfluous. I watched his lips move, but I wasn't really listening from that moment on. I was thinking just how charming he can be, even when he's offering one the loaded revolver. I felt cold and sick. I distinctly remember how wearisome the world seemed as I walked down the steps to the waiting car. My driver spoke to me. That's quite a rare occurrence actually, he's not expected to speak, nor I to answer.

"I hope everything is alright, sir," is what he said.

I purposely did not reply. Pretended not to hear him. Quite illogically, I wondered what he knew. It seems he must merely have read the concern on my face.

I have been unhappy for a while about the position of the Azalea. It does not complement the overall effect of the garden at all. There is something about it I have come to intensely dislike, although I cannot quite say what. Perhaps it is its morbid pallidity.

It came as quite a revelation to me, just how shoddy one's life can be made to appear when exposed to objective scrutiny. It is not at all the Curriculum Vitae one would compose for oneself, although for all intents and purposes it may be closer to the truth. It does tend to make one consider one's worth, question what it was one had been striving to achieve for all those years; that which had seemed much more apparent in the beginning.

But it is the lies which hurt much more than revealed truth can ever do. For every stinging fact, a dozen other libellous, yet nevertheless, damaging "revelations" appeared. Editors of the "popular" press seemed to feel secure from litigation, or at least brave enough to balance the chance of its eventual success against the bonus of increased circulation. In the desire to encourage the feeding frenzy of a scandal hungry readership scant regard was paid to verification of detail, and not only was I made to look an incurable libertine, but also a failure to my office. And this, the latter, hurt by far the most.

I was going to do it there in the potting shed, you know. The Purdey's already loaded. Both barrels. Beautiful piece of craftsmanship that. I had considered the study, but I couldn't have let her face that. All that mess. A policeman once told me that you can never quite clean it all away. All that gore can travel an alarming distance. Spreads all over the place. It doesn't seem right to soil one's home like that. I should imagine it would make it quite inhospitable for future generations. The potting shed is different. You can knock the bloody thing down, I suppose. Burn it. At least there seems some ritual significance to that. Whatever.

I honestly could have done it. I now consider suicide to be the ultimate test of courage. Quite unlike the more popular conception. And believe me, facing it is not at all what they would have you think, either. It doesn't feel like a last act of desperation, quite the contrary. One almost feels noble. It wouldn't have been difficult to go through with it at all, lay those cold barrels in one's mouth, pull the triggers. Kneeling there, though, I wondered if Harriet might not need me, when she came back that is. Have I told you, she used to be so much hardier than I, when we first married? I could see that much in her then, and she proved my judgement to be correct for many years. Appalling though it must sound, perhaps I have been missing something recently, something she's been trying to tell me. What if she'd been quietly calling for help and I never heard? I used to pride myself on being able to read her well. I

68 / *When Harriet Returns*

wonder when that ability left me?

The P.M. should have read my letter by now. He'll be secretly pleased, of course. It saves him the trouble and effort. Couldn't really have left that onerous decision to him. God knows, he's enough problems without mine.

I hope it will all die down soon. I wonder if I could come to terms with being one of the not-so-exclusive club of disgraced ex-politicians. I shall have to learn to look on this as a sort of early retirement.

I really must put away those tools before Harriet returns. Whatever will she think of me. I shall have a whisky when I've finished. I know it's a bit early but I think I've earned a small reward.

It wasn't long after I'd left the garden that the police officers called. A young man and woman. I saw them from the window, speaking with my personal detective as I poured myself a drink. I was just thinking how delightful the Gloxinia looked. Better then ever.

They do go to extraordinary lengths to stress how little your loved ones must have suffered before they died. As if they could know. I could not get over the fact that the young officer repeated this point to me three times when once would have been sufficient. Frightfully burdensome use of the language that boy had too. But I was grateful for his sympathy, he seemed genuinely sincere. Perhaps he hasn't done this sort of thing very often. It was difficult not to be amused by the most disconcerting way his Adam's Apple bobbed about as he talked. I couldn't take my eyes off it. I think I must have stumbled, really, because I found myself in the armchair. The woman officer was picking up the bits of broken whisky glass and placing them gingerly in her unprotected palm. Damn dangerous, that. I advised her to take care. There was an annoying stain on the Axminster that I knew we would never be able to get out. Or should I say I would never be able to get out.

I overheard her saying to my detective that it might be wise to keep an eye on me for a while, the implication being that I might be suffering some sort of shock. He has called for Dr. Pacey to visit me. He has furtively secured the keys to the gin case.

I am about to return to the garden now. I had assumed that, everything being ship-shape, I had finished for the time being. But there is something I have to do in the potting shed.

Robert Graham

Carcasses

Veins turn my stomach. They don't have to be varicose; just visible. Somewhere along the way, I became hardened to decaying flesh. Cellulite holds no further horrors for me. Dimpled, slack, stretched, drooping flesh has been part of life for such a long time. But I can't be doing with veins at all. And the swimming-pool is full of them.

Tuesdays and Thursdays, week in, week out, I swim.

It's free for pensioners then. Nobody looking at us in our clothes could suspect the ugliness hidden beneath. And under the skin – well, who could tell what's there by looking at our undressed carcasses?

Here we are.

There must be fifteen of us on a good day and I know all of them at least by name. Most of us went to the Elementary School together. The streets outside, where we've lived our lives, are dank, Edwardian red-bricks, and it's odd to me that our lifetimes have been passed out there and now we're reaching the end here in the bright, glinting pool, built only five years ago – the day before yesterday, really.

Picture us, crossing and re-crossing the pool – most of us swim widths, not lengths – like sluggardly dredgers passing across a bay.

I'm early today, but I might just as well be late. I don't have any regard for time – I gave it up. There's a clock on the front-room mantelpiece, but that's all. I don't wear a watch.

The blackboard beneath the pool clock says '83°F' in shaky chalk, but it never is. They always say it's that and it's always colder than they say, because 83°F would be warm, wouldn't it?

I'm at the yellow steps, which take you very gradually up to your waist in chilly, sharp blue, but I stop there and look around.

There's Mr. and Mrs. Johnny Weissmuller, as I call them – the diving stars. Neither one of them is any younger than me, but they practise and analyse diving like they were in training for an event. When she completes a dive, never well, he's waiting for her at the side and she'll give him all her attention as he bends from the waist, brings his arms together above his head and gives it some post-match analysis.

70 / *Carcasses*

They're like a pair of teenagers who've just started going with each other. I don't know how she's put up with a lifetime of that.

Johnny nods at me, very formal. Of course, I stretch a big smile back at him.

Nan Morris is in, wading around the shallow end. Her costume's only wet to the waist and there's an empty hollow in it up above, where her right breast should be. I thought they gave you pads to stick in there. I mean, the rest of us have feelings, don't we? Anyway, I don't think Nan's really all there.

I swim a width and turn onto my back to wet my hair. I used to wear a white rubber cap, but I stopped. You wouldn't believe how often I've had people asking about it. Wasn't I wearing a cap anymore? Wasn't I bothered about getting my hair wet? Wouldn't my head be cold without it?

"Look around," I'd tell them. "Are any of this lot dying of pneumonia?"

Worst of them all was Esta McKeever. She went on and on and I held my tongue as long as I could, seeing as her husband had died not long since. She'd had a bad twelve months, really: they'd amputated his right leg at the knee – cancer – in March and by August he was dead anyway.

I turn and begin a length, which brings me along by Gordon, the attendant. He sits in his high-chair, staring without focus and looking like a tennis umpire waiting for a match that's never going to happen. I worry for him. He never acknowledges your presence. She'd never spoken to him before. None of us had. Gordon's very interested in the young girls, especially when they're walking about or waist-high in the water, but not interested in anything else. Today, as he very often is, George is wearing a Coq Sportif tee-shirt. Very fitting.

Jean Mahoney is sat at the other end, so I make a swift turnaround. "Iya," is all I say to Jean.

She can mither on for as long as anyone will let her, given an inch, moaning away about whatever debris floats across her mind: her husband, vandals, semi-skimmed milk, her new diet or the Germans. I can't listen to it anymore, especially not the diet bit. The world has diets on the brain. I mean, where would the British press be without diets and the Royal Family? It makes me sick.

A girl, maybe twenty, shimmies in from the changing rooms. She doesn't even flinch as she passes the draughts from the emergency doors, although that doesn't irritate me as much as her hair. My heart sinks, it's so healthy and strong. I've seen wigs with healthier-looking hair than I've got.

I'm so busy being eaten up by this hair that I don't see Esta McKeever until I'm on top of her.

"Your sonar's not functioning, pet."

"Oh! Sorry, love," I say.

I think a lot about Esta since she became a Born Again. Previous to that, I never had strong feelings about her either way. She was never short of a man when she was a lass and there were those who held that against her. But to me Esta's always been alright. I just never used to think about her like I have since she got God.

I suppose I'd like to believe. I'd like to believe in Father Christmas, too, but I can't anymore. It's hard to remember that far back, but I've a feeling I probably believed in God when I believed in Father Christmas. It was a long time ago.

"Are you stopping or swimming the channel today?" Esta asks. I give a short laugh and settle with my back to the wall. From my new position, I see Mrs. Weismuller enter the water with all the grace of a pantomime cow.

"You're looking well," Esta says.

"I'm not. I look like a transvestite. 'Thou shalt not lie'."

"'Build each other up'."

"Eh?"

"What Paul said."

"Paul who?"

"Paul who yourself. We're having a special charity lunch at church on Sunday. Would you like to come at all?"

"No I would not."

"The idea is third world food at first world prices and all the money goes to the hungry in Africa."

"Did it ever cross your mind that if God wanted people in Africa to eat better, He'd send them a McDonalds?"

Esta looks at me with patient good humour. She's used to me.

"There's enough food in the world for everyone, but God leaves us to sort it out. Free will, you see."

"So God depends on the likes of you to do His work for Him? You'd think He could do better."

"Oh no. It's not a question of ability. It's availability that counts."

"You're like a parrot, you." It really gets me the way she spills out these polished phrases she's picked up at church. "There's no way I could go to your church. I'd need subtitles to understand what they were saying."

Esta laughs and tells me she supposes I'm right. Quite disarming – it's a knack she has.

Jean Mahoney floats up to us. With her red goggles and green and orange cap, she's a sight.

"I'n't it cold?" she says, and I can see that we're trapped here at the deep end.

"I'm sorry about Rover," Esta says.

"Aye, it's all very sad . . ."

"What about Rover?" I ask. Esta is shaking her head at me.

"Put down," says Jean. "He were hit by the lemonade lorry, a week past on Thursday. It were the kindest thing, really."

"You'll miss him," Esta says.

"Oh, I will . . ."

Some lengths later, Esta floats up to me on her back. She doesn't do backstroke, exactly. She just kicks herself along, lying on her back, no arms, a bit like the Venus de Milo chucked in a pool.

There's a silence. We both sit with our backs to the wall in the shallow end. I nod at Johnny Weismuller and his missus.

"She's like a sea elephant."

Esta says nothing. I've noticed this about her.

"Oh come on. It's not exactly character assassination."

"'The wicked will not inherit the Kingdom of God,' Paul says in Corinthians. 'Neither idolaters, nor thieves, nor slander –"

"Spare me. You Christians are all the same," I tell her. "You think you're the only ones that know owt about goodness. Do you think God's bothered whether or not I make a remark about the Weismullers' diving club?"

"Since you mention it, I think He worries about *every*thing."

"Oh well," I say, "I wouldn't know as much about Him as *you*, Esta."

"You could if you wanted to."

Carcasses / 73

"Well, I *don't* want to."

I don't understand how these things get started. It just happens.

"I'm sorry you feel that way," Esta says. And she is – you can tell.

"*Don't* be."

And I swim off.

As I slowly make my way towards the deep end, I'm feeling more upset than I ought to be. I'm going over and over how God is alright for those that can believe in Him. For the rest of us, He's like a luxury item: it looks nice in the shop window, but you know you'll never be able to have it for yourself.

And I'm angry with Esta for being pleasant when I'm pushing her not to be and for wanting to do what's right.

I'm still thinking about this when I turn for another length and see Johnny Weismuller dive off the side and plunge perfectly into the water. He surfaces and powers towards the middle of the pool. Here Esta is doing her Venus de Milo impression. Johnny reaches her in a few, fluid strokes. I'm wondering what's going on. He stops and stands by her in the water. I keep swimming towards them.

"Oh no!" Johnny shouts in his mahogany voice.

At this, Gordon the attendant springs from his high chair, takes two dancer's steps and dives in, fully clothed. When I reach Esta, Gordon has just pulled up beside her and lowered his feet to the pool floor.

"There's nothing you can do," Johnny tells him. "There's nothing anyone can do."

"What?" I say.

I can see Esta, laid out on the water, her eyes stopped still, fixed on the ceiling. I can see a pink flush in them, lots of little pink capillaries, and I think you can't be dead and have bloodshot eyes.

"But she was just – " I say.

"I know," Johnny says. "I know."

I'm thinking he has watched too many people dying in films for his own good and I'm thinking that it's maybe my fault, that I *upset* her to death. I'm as surprised as he is to find myself whimpering in Johnny Weismuller's arms.

*

Later, in the showers, I'm stood in the too-hot torrent which drills into my shoulders. There's a full quota of carcasses in there: me and three others, each standing like a waxwork, silent.

In my mind, I see her floating and wonder how many yards she drifted after she'd gone, how long it was before Johnny made his epic dive. I wonder if Esta's soul just left the swimming pool and went straight to God, or was she disappointed at the end?

I go on thinking about it.

Gary Webb

The Strange Case of Marie Annette

Behind a locked door in the private place of a cool, still, pastel-coloured room, a nice lady, intent on re-enacting a performance, runs the erectile tip of her tongue over her top lip as she jerks open a pair of long, wide red and white striped curtains. Strips of sunlight stream into the room and the only other occupant of the room, a nervous little girl uncomfortably seated on the edge of a green fabric couch, blinks and winks excitedly. The nice lady advances toward the girl. As she moves closer, the nice lady shakes her long raven hair free from its stern tied up restraint. Arriving by the girl, she arches her back and straightens her tight navy blue suit skirt by brushing her palms firmly down over her broad hips. She then bends and wriggles her contours into the accommodating creaking black leather of a swivel chair, positioned up against the couch, the arms touching.

"Come on, Marie, sweetheart, we'll do it together. Try and tell me what happened at the show. Tell me about Mr. Punch," asks the nice, power-dressed, well-spoken lady, sitting cross-legged, her right calf muscle splayed flat against her left leg and her glasses precariously perched at the end of her nose.

"Mr. Punch was naughty," answers the little girl in a high pitched voice.

"What did he do, lovely?" asks the nice, smartly-dressed, well-spoken, lavender-smelling lady. At the thought of this, the little girl screws up her face to sob for the end of the world. She gushes her words and grips her constant companion of a well-bashed, one-armed, flaxen-haired dolly tightly to the breast of her *Thunderbirds* T-shirt.

"He hurt . . . those people. He hit them! He killed them!" The nice lady leans over, creaking the leather of her chair, to the soft and soothing green-coloured couch where Marie sits. The padded left shoulder of her navy blue suit jacket rises as she reaches over to stroke the little girl's straight, red-ribbon tied, blonde pony-tail hair. She gives Marie a soft kiss on the forehead and asks her again to try and remember. The little girl begins her story, calmer than she was, but still sniffing, and gulping the occasional word.

"Mr. Punch came home late at night. He couldn't get into the house. Judy locked him out 'cos he'd been drinking."

"Who was Judy?" asks the nice lady, uncrossing her legs, with

76 / *The Strange Case of Marie Annette*

little clicks of friction from her flesh-coloured stockings, and tapping the enamel of her even white teeth with a pencil end.

"Judy was the mummy."

"And was naughty Mr. Punch the daddy?"

"Yes."

"Carry on, sweetheart."

"He shouted through the letterbox: 'Hip pip poy! Hip pip poy! Hip pip poy! I'm coming, I'm coming, I'm coming. I won't be a minute!' Then Mr. Punch smacked the door in and Judy ran upstairs to save her baby and . . .'' At this point the lady brusquely interrupts and asks: "How old was the baby?"

"Four," replies Marie, without hesitation.

"Boy or girl?"

"A little girl."

"Carry on please." Marie begins to speak faster. More intensely. Her moist brown eyes widen, dry and harden with a glint of insanity. As she pours the words out she stares at the visible nothings that appear in corners of rooms in moments of private desperation.

". . . And Judy locked herself and her baby in her bedroom and . . . and Mr. Punch charged up the stairs and . . . and he was shouting and shouting: 'Here I am, here I am, here I am. Judy, Judy, Ju-dy. Where are you?' and Mr. Punch kicked open all the doors until he found where Judy and . . . and the baby were hiding."

The lady again leans over and softly strokes back into place the strands of blonde hair that are sticking to Marie's sweat-beaded and furrowed brow. The girl takes a deep breath and relaxes a little. She asks for a cigarette and drops her dolly to take one that protrudes from the open flip-top packet offered by the lady. He hand trembles and she has trouble introducing the speckled brown filter to her glossy lips. As her lips purse to hold the cigarette, her head moves forward and, in a slightly muffled voice from the side of her mouth, she asks for a light. The lady looks at those lips as she stretches over to click up an orange flame from her gold Ronson lighter, and she frowns at the disturbing mental picture she is beginning to form.

Marie drags deeply at the tobacco and relaxes a little more. Nothing is said between the girl and lady for a few moments. In the stillness, both watch a nicotine genie rise vertically, gradually take a shape, look down contemptuously on those who released him, and curl off towards the lamp in the centre of the ochre-stained

The Strange Case of Marie Annette / 77

ceiling, highlighted in and out of his journey by the streams of diagonal sunlight from the window. Marie continues, in a deeper voice:

"Before Mr. Punch kicked the bedroom door in, Judy hid the baby under the bed. When he was through the door, Mr. Punch moved toward Judy and said: 'kissie, kissie, kissie.' Judy tried to avoid Mr. Punch's mouth. She protested that he stank of beer and whisky. But he just got more aggressive. He said: 'Now, Judy, we will have a little dance.' He grabbed her waist and swirled Judy around the bedroom. Then Mr. Punch stopped. 'Where's the baby?' he asked Judy. Judy said nothing. 'Go on, go on, go and get the baby!' demanded Mr. Punch. Judy reluctantly got the baby from under the bed and gave it to Mr. Punch. Mr. Punch held the baby. The baby began to cry. 'Go and get my tea ready,' Mr. Punch told Judy. 'Fry me some sausages!' he ordered. Judy went down to the kitchen. Mr. Punch played roughly with the baby. The baby still cried."

Between the staccato sentences, Marie pushes her shoulders back and her firm, unfettered breasts forward as she takes deep and regular draws on the cigarette. She does it properly; from experience. Inhaling slowly and deliberately, holding, swallowing and exhaling sharply through her stud-pierced nose. She continues:

"Mr. Punch couldn't stop the baby crying. He was losing his temper. He shouted at the baby: 'Oh, you naughty girl, you naughty girl, you naughty little rascal!' Judy heard and came running back to her baby. The couple struggled, both pulling at the little girl as though she were a rag doll. They pulled so hard they broke the little girl's arm and she cried even louder." Marie takes her right hand – with the cigarette between her fore and middle fingers – and rubs her left arm at the elbow joint

"Who won the struggle?" asks the lady. Marie stubs out her cigarette.

"Mr. Punch won the struggle. Judy ran downstairs and came back up with a baseball bat. She screamed at Mr. Punch to leave the baby alone. She told him if he touched me ever again she'd kill him."

The nice lady psychiatrist sits up, pushes her glasses to the bridge of her nose and pencils the word 'progress' on to her notepad. Her woman patient begins to rock back and forth, rubbing her moist palms up and down along the skin-tight blue denim that stretches

78 / *The Strange Case of Marie Annette*

over her strong thighs, and continues, slipping back into a high pitched voice:

"Then daddy threw me aside and attacked mummy. I crawled under the bed." Marie gushes and stutters and stops and gushes and stutters again as she speaks. "Mummy hit daddy with the bat . . . . daddy t-took it from mummy . . . . daddy p-pulled mummy's hair . . . . daddy p-pulled mummy onto the floor . . . . mummy b-begged daddy not to . . . . daddy b-beat mummy's brains in."

Marie pauses for a moment, stops rocking and rubbing and composes herself, then continues in her deeper voice:

"'*That's* the way to do it,' my father said, softly, over my mother's lifeless body. At the open front doorway the bell was ringing and there was shouting: 'Are you all right? Is everybody all right?' Our neighbours: the Chinaman and the African, had heard the trouble and called a policeman and a doctor. They came in, cautiously, one behind the other, the policeman leading. Father had gone downstairs and was crouching behind the broken front door, hidden and waiting for them. I'd crept to the bannister and was peeking between the rails. When they came within arm's reach, father attacked them. He hit each one on the head very hard and very quickly. They all dropped down bleeding and lay remarkably quiet. Their limbs involuntarily twitched, for a while. 'That's the way to do it!' father said, again. Soon, more police arrived and arrested my father. This time without a struggle. I watched him hang for mass murder. I stopped crying then, I haven't cried since, until now. I shan't cry again. May I have another cigarette?"

Later, the psychiatrist reports her progress to a white-coated, German-accented male professor.

"Well, Herr Professor Anderson, I regressed the woman patient . . ." the psychiatrist hesitates for a moment and consults her notepad, "a Miss Marie Annette Doll, back to her childhood, spent at the Skegness Butlin's camp, and gradually got her to relive the deaths of her parents."

"A mozt difficult caze, Doctor Corbett," the professor comments. "Ein infant experienzing zix deaths, tvize a day, efery day – veather permitting – for the length of a zummer zeason at ein Englander zeaside stalag, could haf become a mozt dizturbed adult. Waz der a pozzible zexual connotation in the zauzages, ja!?"

"No, Herr Professor. It's part of the play."

"Ah zo, pity. But you English are zo zuppressed. Did I efer tell

The Strange Case of Marie Annette / 79

chauffeur's big, pink, zix-veel bratwurst? That vas a real doozy."

"No, Herr Professor, but I did once unravel a potentially disastrous *ménage à trois* between two flowerpot men and a weed. Do you remember the 'Flubalubaglub Paraquat Case'?" asks the psychiatrist, proudly.

"Oh ja, ja. Vell, anyvay, Zylvia," responds the professor, somewhat deflated, "back to the caze in hand. Do you feel the patient iz zootably cured unt ready to go into the vorld unt take her plaze among the other puppetz unt find gainful employment?"

"Most definitely, Herr Professor. In fact we've already found her a job, and, although there are strings attached, I'm sure she'll be the most well adjusted puppet on the show. The very spitting image of . . ."

Kathleen Jones

Glass

Lately it's begun to bother me that my life has become so exclusively female. The little red notebook beside the phone has line upon line of women's names in it. My own friends, mother's of my daughter's friends. When I go into the bathroom the shelves are loaded with soap, bottles of bath oil, exfoliant gel, anti-wrinkle cream, the girl's zit lotions and eye shadows, and the cabinet bulges with what my mother would have discreetly called 'women's things'.

Men no longer whistle at me from building sites. Girl friends ring me up to invite me to all-women dinner parties where we eat vegetarian high fibre food and discuss our ex-husbands. Men are people you pass in the street, faces on television, always with someone else in wine bars on Saturday night.

I remember when I was a child, my mother had two unmarried friends called Doreen and Sue, who lived chaste, unimaginable and (she somehow managed to imply) pointless lives without men. They lived in an Edwardian semi with Doreen's elderly mother. They had both been engaged during the war, but one fiancée had been killed at Tobruk and the other went off with a girl in the WRACS.

Doreen was a senior civil servant with short masculine hair and a series of elegantly cut grey suits with permanently pleated skirts. She had oddly sexy legs, smooth and hairless in sheer nylons, and tiny feet she pampered with hand-made leather shoes. Sue had taken up offers of training after the war and become a dentist. She was very plump and made her own dresses in bizarre fabrics that looked like furnishing material. She was lazy and comfortable and had thick blonde fluff on her upper lip she never bothered to remove.

They came into our lives on Bank Holiday weekends, evicting me from my bedroom to sleep on a shake-down on the floor. They brought my mother unaffordable Elizabeth Arden cosmetics in presentation caskets, malt whisky for my father and once they gave me the triple-layered net petticoat my mother had refused to buy. They would sit at the table in our bare, functional kitchen after lunch, smoking cigarettes and drinking Amaretto with their coffee. The bottle had pictures of Italy on the label and a coy looking cupid in a medallion around the neck. They giggled over mutual memories, talked about politics, books, Hollywood gossip, the war. They did everything together, shopping, theatre, art galleries, holidays in France. Such a pity, my mother used to say when they'd gone. Such a waste.

I asked my friend Kate, who always seems to have a lover, "How do you meet men?"

"I don't know," she said. "It just happens." The last one was an artist. She admired a painting and it turned out to be one of his and he said why don't we go for a coffee and that was it.

I look at myself in the mirror. Thirty something. Divorced. Three children. It stares back at me. All that history written in the little lines trawling my neck, the anxious tightening round the eyes, the softening outline and lengthening vision.

Kate on the other hand – twice married, two children, mid forties – is tall and magpie coloured, her face grooved like a record of everything she's ever done, and always in black clothes pinned together with bits of jumble sale diamante where the zips have gone. She looks dangerous. Perhaps that's what men go for.

I once tried it. Shoving my hair back in an old fifties turban and putting on a post-war crêpe de chine dress with a dipping hem and one of those full-skirted coats with a velvet collar and nipped waist that had belonged to my mother. But I looked as though I was auditioning for amateur theatricals, so I gave the clothes to Kate.

My last encounter with a man was at an evening class. I went to learn how to make terrariums out of bits of glass and lead. It had seemed a good idea at the time to learn some kind of useful craft, and I imagined them full of green plants reflecting underwater light on the window sills of my flat. I planned to give them to friends for Christmas. The shapes of coloured glass, diamonds, squares, and hexagons of blue and wave-green, were beautiful. They had a satisfying scrunch as the cutter bit through the glass. But afterwards I cut my fingers on the rough edges and found it difficult to line them up for soldering.

The man sitting at the bench next to me used to help. He would stand behind me and put his arms over mine to hold the pieces while I moved the soldering iron down the edge. He smelt of wool and skin and hair. Natural – not cosmetic – things. He was interested in glass, he said. His grandfather had been a glass blower in Ireland. He said he dreamed of taking early retirement and having a stained glass workshop.

One night he rang up. "I hope you don't mind," he said, "but it's my fiftieth birthday." He called it the Big Five Oh. "I'm on my own," he went on, "and I wondered if you'd come out and help me celebrate?"

He had always seemed friendly and pleasant, so I said yes. The girls were very excited about my date. They supervised my make-up and hair and dragged out my blue dress from the back of the wardrobe. It's out of fashion, but I've kept it because of the colour. It's a happy dress, the girls tell me, a lucky dress. But they have romantic ideas imbibed from picture papers and American teenage novels.

He'd arranged to meet me at a small French bistro near his flat. I refused the cocktails he pressed on me, preferring to stick to sherry. I know where I am with sherry. He was drinking whisky, doubles, and he ordered an extra large bottle of wine with his meal. "We might as well enjoy ourselves," he said, "and we don't have to stagger very far afterwards if we do have a 'touche' (he pronounced it the French way making a little measuring gesture with his fingers) to much to drink." And he laughed.

The menu was unbelievable. My eyes lingered greedily on the prawns in pernod, the peppered steak flambéd in brandy, the chicken breasts in cream and lemon. I ordered some deep fried Camembert as a starter, little crisp brown buttons with a soft, creamy interior.

He was noisier and more expansive than he'd been at evening classes. During the meal he kept touching me, little gratuitous points of contact as he passed the wine, the accidental brush of knee under the table.

I asked him about himself. He was in insurance apparently, posted here temporarily for nine months or so. His real home was in Devon. He went back there at weekends 'to refuel'. As he talked I could see his unmentioned wife hovering over his shoulder, washing his immaculate shirts, prising the pieces of solder out of his hand-knitted jumpers in the immaculate detached house he described overlooking the Tamar. Her whole existence confirmed by the single indiscreet 'we' he used when talking about a planned holiday in Spain.

I glanced down at my plate. The waiter was serving my steak au poivre on a bed of shiny red pimentos grinning up like a row of vaginas. My head was saying 'he's a creep', but my body was saying 'he's not wholly repulsive and he really fancies you'. The steak was very thick between my teeth, crusted with pepper and mustard and the rich juices trickled down my throat. A little flame, mustard and the rich juices trickled down my throat. A little flame, lit by the wine, had begun to burn at the base of my spine. Very few of Kate's men friends would have been able to afford a meal like this. Last year it had been a climber she'd met when doing a bit of topless sunbathing in a secluded spot at the top of the Avon Gorge. He'd heaved himself over a pinnacle of rock and landed right beside her in a clatter of pitons. He was at least twenty years younger than her. "So what," Kate said. "I'm not intending to settle down with him for life. Anyway, who wants all that droopy middle-aged flab in bed with you? I've plenty of my own."

I looked across the table at his polished forehead, where the hair was receding, and the expense-account bulge under his shirt and wondered what it would be like.

It was raining when we left the restaurant after an enormous bill he'd settled with his Diner's card. I wondered how he'd explain that to his wife, and whether he would claim me against expenses for business entertaining. A skittish east wind had blown up. We both shivered and I clutched my wool coat tighter round my neck. "Is there room for two under that coat?" he joked, putting his arm round me.

In the restaurant he'd asked if I would go round to his flat for a night cap. He had a bottle of champagne in the fridge for the occasion, he said, and he wanted me to see the three terrariums he'd completed, all planted up. When he took early retirement, he said, he might go into business selling them. "What about your wife?" I asked. He paused, then shrugged. "My wife and I live on different tracks," he said, "I go my way and she goes hers. It's understood."

"By whom?" I asked.

He walked me home and we stood on the doorstep, like middle-aged teenagers and I explained that I couldn't ask him in because of the girls. He kissed the soft skin on the inside of my lips and touched my breasts and hair with practised hands. Stupid with wine and food and sexual desire, I could feel my body respond to these terrible, unwanted caresses, programmed by wretched biology. "No strings," he said in my ear, "just fun. You wouldn't regret it."

When I was young I used to imagine Doreen and Sue to be perpetually virgin and think how awful it must be. Later, married, I wondered about their ambiguous relationship.

Then, a few years ago, when Doreen died of cancer, my mother

84 / Glass

went to pack up her belongings and take them down to Oxfam. Sue couldn't bear to touch them. Wouldn't even go into her room. At the back of a drawer my mother found a box of letters from one of Doreen's colleagues, another senior civil servant. He was married, but couldn't divorce his wife because of his position, or so he said. They had, apparently, met for lunch every day, written to each other, and once they had gone to Italy, to Tuscany, for a holiday. They were beautiful letters, my mother told me on the phone, so full of loving. "Such a pity," she said, "Such a waste."

My favourite fantasy before drifting off to sleep is the one where I meet a New Man – the kind that are never free because other women are hanging on to them like mad. He takes me out, sometimes to an expensive restaurant on the river, or to the opera. I'm wearing a dress I once saw in a boutique in Clifton, jade green and turquoise squares of silk weighted with tiny tassels of glass beads. He drives me home in his open-topped car and we make love under beech trees in a field. Sometimes I alter it slightly and he's in one of the caring professions with holes in his sweaters and we sit at a pavement cafe counting the pennies in our pocket linings. But the end is always the same.

Yesterday Kate rang me up to invite me to supper. "No men." she said. "I'm giving them up." She's just spent a week in Amsterdam. "A mistake," she said. "I thought – him being an artist . . . but I never seem to learn. Why do we do it?" she asked.

The off-licence had some Amaretto in a green glass bottle with coloured pictures of Italy on the label. Cupid, in his medallion on the neck band, aimed the arrow with a menacing gesture – sending out the call sign we all seem programmed to read. I ran my finger gently down the long neck of the bottle, seeing the green eye of the liquid inside reflecting the room's light across the counter.

I bought some to take to Kate's.

Stephen Bohl

Dinosaur

Angelo went into the toyshop and spoke to the young assistant behind the counter. "Hello. Can I see the three Rex's in the window, please?"

The young woman hesitated for a second and stared: long enough to take in the well-worn denims, Italianate ringlets, shadow of stubble, the silver skull and crossbones earring dangling from Angelo's left ear, and . . . something else. Something deeper, something peculiar, something skew whiff. Angelo caught the flicker of suspicion behind the young woman's eyes. He had seen that look a thousand times. He ignored it. He didn't care. He just wanted to see the dinosaurs.

The girl moved over to the window and leant over the partition to retrieve the Rex's. "All three of them?" she asked.

"Yeah."

Angelo had a good look at her as she bent over the stomach height partition. He liked what he saw.

The girl stood upright, and turned, clutching the three plastic Tyrannosaurii Rex. There was one blue one, a brown one and a green one. Each was about nine inches tall, with a gaping red oral cavity lined with savage white teeth, stumpy fixed forearms ending in small claws, moveable chunky hind legs, and all rounded off with a long thick tail tapering to a point. The girl handed the toys to Angelo. He took them, then perplexed the already perplexed looking assistant by asking for a mirror.

"A mirror?"

"Yes please."

The young woman's eyes flickered suspiciously again. She stood for a second looking at Angelo, then went off to the back of the shop to look for a mirror.

Looking after her, Angelo now saw that there was someone else in the shop. At the back, in what looked like a stockroom, lurked an older woman who Angelo assumed must be the manageress. As the young assistant disappeared into the stockroom hissing nervously, "He wants a mirror", the manageress stepped forward, and flashed a thin forced smile quickly at Angelo, before walking to the counter to take up her station behind it.

Angelo looked amused. Mainly because he was.

The shop assistant returned with the mirror: a circular double-

86 / *Dinosaur*

sided one about the size of Angelo's head. Angelo took the mirror, then perplexed the shop assistant and manageress even more than he had done already by holding it in front of his face, and holding each of the plastic lizards in turn above his head, while peering intently into the glass to see how they looked. He tried all three, then pulled a face. He put the mirror down on the counter together with the dinosaurs.

"No good," he said. "I can't see. Have you got a full length mirror?"

The shop assistant now looked distinctly worried. Her eyes wide, she shook her head.

Angelo pondered for a second. Then his eyes lit up. "They've got one next door!" he said. "In the jewellery shop." He scooped up the three Rex's in one arm and was off. "Come on" he shouted, over his shoulder. "You come with me. I won't run off."

The shop assistant opened her mouth to protest, but Angelo was already half way out the door. She looked helplessly at the manageress, who looked helplessly after Angelo, before collecting her thoughts and ushering the girl quickly out of the shop. "Stay with him," demanded the manageress.

Angelo was waiting outside, the three plastic toys all held in one bedenimed arm.

"OK?" he said. He turned without waiting for an answer and strode to the door of Gazebo, a hippy jewellery, clothes and fancy goods shop. Angelo pushed his way in. "Can we just use your mirror?"

The bead-burdened girl behind the counter, silently and with slightly furrowed brow, indicated the mirror with one arm. The toyshop assistant smiled apologetically at the hippy girl, then followed Angelo to the mirror, warily, like a cat stalking a dog, ready to fly up the nearest tree should the quarry so much as turn its head.

Angelo stood in front of the full length mirror and tried the three dinosaurs in turn, holding each three inches above his head. "That's better," he said. "I can see what they look like now." the two staff in the shop and their solitary customer watched incredulously. The customer laughed. The toyshop assistant hovered nervously, shrivelled with embarrassment.

"Definitely the green," said Angelo. "What do you think?" He held the green Tyrannosaurus above his head and turned to the toyshop assistant. She could manage only a thin smile and a stiff nod. Angelo smirked. The young woman was staring at him with eyes like saucers.

"Thank you," said Angelo to the Gazebo staff as he walked out the door. Still silent, they watched him go. The toyshop assistant scuttled hurriedly after him. She couldn't get out fast enough.

Back in the toyshop, Angelo put all three dinosaurs down on the counter and announced that he would take the green one. He pulled a fiver from the pocket of his denim jacket. The manageress pulled a large brown paper bag from under the counter, picked up the green Rex and made as if to put it in.

"Don't bother," said Angelo. "I'll wear it."

The manageress simply stared at him.

"The Rex, not the bag," explained Angelo.

The manageress remained stock still with the dinosaur in one hand and the paper bag in the other. The girl shop assistant stared at Angelo with the widest eyes that anybody has yet managed to have in the history of the world.

"Joke," said Angelo, and laughed.

Betraying no further visible reaction, the manageress slipped the plastic reptile inside the bag, took Angelo's money, and handed him the bag.

She handed him his change.

"Thank you," said Angelo, brightly.

"Thank *you*," murmured the manageress.

Angelo walked home.

Back at his bedsit, Angelo put the plastic Rex down on his table then went to the drawer of the sideboard and fished out an untidy coil of wire coathangers which he'd been saving.

He sat at his table, then fashioned two of the coathangers into a harness to fit around his head which, fixed at the ears, would hold the dinosaur erect above his scalp.

Still sat at the table, Angelo crowned himself with the whole contraption, then went to the mirror to view the results. Perfect! The wire headpiece held the nine inch plastic lizard three inches above his head, absolutely upright: vitally vertical. It looked great. Angelo shook his head quickly from side to side. His contraption was completely secure. He'd thought he might need to tie it on with some string or elastic bands. But it worked perfectly as it was. Comfortable too. Excellent.

88 / *Dinosaur*

Might as well set off straight away.

As Angelo stepped from the front door heading for the street, he hummed happily to himself. He was looking forward to this. It was going to be fun.

He only encountered two people on his way to the bus stop. They were an elderly couple with a shopping trolley. They just stood by the wall and watched him go past, peering myopically up at the Rex like a pair of mildly curious moles. Angelo had been hoping for a slightly more animated response. Still, it was early days yet.

The next people that Angelo encountered were two teenage girls sat at the bus stop. They stared as Angelo approached, then burst out laughing when they saw what he'd got on his head. As Angelo came towards them they nudged each other and goggled, trying not to look, then turning back for one more peek. Angelo reckoned they were about sixteen. Arriving at the bus stop he flashed them his most winning smile, and winked. The two girls clammed up and faced front, resolutely ignoring him. Angelo was disappointed. He'd fancied a chat. The blonde, in particular, was a cutie.

As they waited in silence for the bus, Angelo thought he heard a snicker or two, and looked round hopefully; but he found the girls each time staring coldly frontwards, poker-faced.

Various people walking past on the opposite side of the road stopped to point across at Angelo, then laugh or look puzzled. This cheered him up somewhat. At least he was getting some attention.

When the bus arrived Angelo let the two girls get on first. The bus driver scowled when he saw Angelo, but he didn't say anything.

"City centre, please," said Angelo. He paid his fare. As he walked to the stairs he observed with satisfaction the various reactions of passengers on the lower deck: amusement, bafflement, hostility, grimaces of bored disapproval from 'seen it all before' types.

Angelo went upstairs and took his seat as the bus crawled up Oxford Road.

An elderly man sat in front of Angelo across the aisle was looking back at him, a look of amusement on his face.

"Aimez-vous ma chappeau?" said Angelo.

"Mon chappeau," corrected the man.

"Mon chappeau."

"Yes. It's very nice. Is it rag week?"

"No."

Dinosaur / 89

"Is it a publicity stunt?"
"Yes."
"What are you publicising?"
"Me."
The man laughed good-naturedly and faced front again. Angelo smiled.

He got off the bus in Piccadilly. He headed for Market Street, the main shopping precinct. Angelo moved through the throng as people gasped with amusement, pointed, looked confused, disgusted, or disinterested. Whatever, within seconds of getting off the bus, Angelo found himself the centre of attention, stared at by hundreds, many of them awe-struck, mouths agog, pulling at their neighbours' sleeves. This was brilliant. He should have thought of this before. He'd turned every head in the street. Almost. He was a star. An instant celebrity. People laughed as he approached. Angelo grinned at them.

He suddenly found himself surrounded by a gang of street urchins, all boys aged eight to ten. They attached themselves to him, trailing along behind and beside him. Angelo heard the twitter of cat-calls, but ignored it. Then the leader of the band, a square-headed thug-faced ten year old in a red Man. United top, stuck his face round in front of Angelo and squinted up at him:

"Are you a nutter or what?"
"What."
"I said are you a nutter?"
"I said I'm a what."
"You are a nutter."
"Mais non. I'm a Pisces."
"You what? You a friggin' headcase?"
"Is the pope a dentist?"
"Eh?"
"Are you a bird-bath?"
The boy pulled his ugly face into a look of disgust. "Twat," he explained to his friends. He stopped walking. His feral troupe stopped with him.

"What's the square root of a cabbage?" asked Angelo, looking back.

"Div," shouted the boy half-heartedly after him. Angelo saluted. He was glad they'd got bored so quickly.

He continued to Market Street. The first thing he saw when he

90 / *Dinosaur*

got there was a TV reporter and cameraman doing a vox pop, interviewing people while they did their shopping. The reporter, who Angelo recognised from the local news programme, looked up, saw him, and pointed. The next thing Angelo saw was the reporter and her cameraman flying towards him like supersonic moths captivated by a spotlight.

"We're from BBC NorthWest," said the reporter straight away. "We're asking people what they think of the Maastricht Treaty. Have you heard of it? May we interview you for the show?"

"Sure."

"Okay?"

"Yeah."

The reporter nodded to the cameraman. He lifted his camera in readiness, then began filming. The reporter spoke into her microphone.

"What do you think the Maastricht Treaty means to the people of the North West?"

"Nothing," said Angelo.

"Okay," the reporter said to her cameraman. He lowered his camera.

"Is that it?" said Angelo. "I do know about Maastricht, you know: European unity, ERM, monetary union, subsidiarity and all that. I'm a Nietzschean on Europe. I think it should be one big Euro-state, then we could all stop bickering and having wars."

"No, that's all right," said the reporter. "That's all we need. What's your name?"

"Deano," said Angelo. The cameraman laughed.

"Deano what?"

"Deano Shaw." The cameraman laughed again. The woman reporter looked at Angelo, waiting.

"Dean Shaw," lied Angelo.

"Right. Why have you got that dinosaur on your head?"

"What dinosaur?"

The cameraman laughed again.

"Will it be on tonight?" asked Angelo.

"Yes," said the reporter. "If they use it."

The reporter and her cameraman went off to interview someone else.

Angelo walked to the glass doors of the Arndale indoor shopping centre and went in. He headed for W.H. Smith's. He enjoyed his latest round of people laughing, gawping, scowling. He moved past them all with a regal stately air, head and dinosaur erect. A prince of the realm. The realm of the mad. Except I'm not mad, thought Angelo.

"Are you a nutter or what?" squawked a voice down at thigh height, rousing him from his musings. He looked down at two thirteen year old girls, potential older sisters of the male gang he'd encountered earlier. They were perched on the low lip of the ornamental pond outside Smith's. It was the saddest looking ornamental pond Angelo had ever seen – just a concrete oblong with a tiled bottom, containing three inches of discoloured water and some green pennies. The pond was supposed to be a fountain, but the bare pipe at its centre, one foot high, could manage no more than a pathetic dribble. A dustbin would have been more picturesque; or more colourful, at least.

Another strident squawk drew Angelo's attention to the fact that one of the thirteen year olds was demanding satisfaction.

"Oi, div, I'm talking to you. Are you a nutter or what?"

Angelo smiled. "Non, je ne suis pas un Nut-err," said Angelo, heavily exaggerating the accent on the final franglais word.

"You what?"

"No, I am not a nutter," Angelo translated.

"So why 'ave you got that dinosaur on your 'ead?"

"'Cos I'd look pretty daft with a dinosaur on my knee, wouldn't I?"

"Yeah," said the girl sarcastically.

"Are you a mate of that cowboy?" said the second girl, with the same strident squawk as her friend.

"What cowboy?"

"The nutter who comes down here in his cowboy gear, with the radio. You his mate?"

"Don't know him," said Angelo.

"He's always here," said the girls. "He goes round talking to 'imself and grinning, and carrying his radio. He walks really fast. He has these cap-guns, –"

The girl broke off and started laughing, looking at something behind Angelo. Her friend did the same.

Angelo felt a tap on his shoulder. He turned to find himself face to face with the very person the girl had just been speaking of: the mad cowboy. He was pointing a toy pistol at Angelo. Angelo looked

92 / *Dinosaur*

at it, then up at a taut, brown, weather-beaten face, wide eyes and a mouth which grinned desperately and permanently beneath a toy cowboy hat much too small for its owner's head. Besides the hat, the man was squeezed into a boy's cowboy waistcoat, and sported twin toy gunbelts and a second silver cap gun to match the one levelled at Angelo's stomach. The man was five inches shorter than Angelo and extremely skinny. Angelo smiled at him.

"Buzz off," said the cowboy.

Angelo looked at him. "Why?"

"'Cos I said so. You're on my patch. I'm a madman. I'm the maddest and the baddest. I'm madder than you." He was about as frightening as a box of tissues. A loon maybe, but a madman, never.

"Ah!" said Angelo, raising an instructive finger. "But if you *think* you're mad you probably aren't."

"I am mad," protested the cowboy. "Watch this." He stepped over the lip of the ornamental pond and stood in its dismal tray of water. Then he stood looking back at Angelo, slack-jawed and expectant.

"We can all do that," said Angelo.

"Go on then."

"I don't want to get my feet wet."

"I win then."

"Win what?"

The cowboy stepped out of the pool, his cheap training shoes sodden and dripping.

"Come on, get it off." He waved his pistol at Angelo's head. "I'm the only madman around here. I'm the maddest and the baddest. I'll go crazy on yer," he warned. "You're –". Whoops. Angelo suddenly whipped the dinosaur and harness off his head and held them behind his back, as he looked past the crazy cowpoke. He'd spotted someone he knew: Ruth, a friend of his sister's and his next Big Hope.

Angelo skirted quickly around the cowboy.

"Oi," protested Mr. Way Out West.

"Sod off," said Angelo.

Ruth hadn't seen him yet. Angelo deftly deposited the dinosaur and coathangers in a convenient bin as he passed.

"Hi, Ruth," he said.

"Hi."

She was a member of his sister's lacrosse club, and one of the prettiest. Angelo fancied his chances with her at the next lacrosse club "do".

"What are you doing?"

"Just some shopping," she said.

"Bought anything nice?"

"Not really. Just a few things. What are you doing?"

"Er, shopping."

"Have you bought anything?"

"No, they didn't have it."

"They didn't have what?"

"Er, a tape. Are you going to dance with me at the next lacrosse club do?"

"Um. Yes. If I go. Well, must dash. I'm meeting my sister."

"Right. See you soon."

"Bye."

Angelo caught the bus home. He was happy after his success with Ruth, but in a flap. No way now did he want his 'interview' to be on the local news tonight; or any night. His outlook had changed.

Six-thirty that evening, Angelo was there in front of the telly on tenterhooks watching North West Tonight: their most attentive viewer ever. The programme featured a piece on Maastricht including interviews with people on the street, but not the one with him, thank Christ. What a let off. Angelo sighed with relief. The last thing he wanted now was for Ruth to see him on telly in Market Street wearing a green plastic dinosaur on his head.

Wendy Robertson

Passion

When they started talking about the closing of the last pit, weeping and wailing like they did, I started to think about another thing which is vanishing: that thing those men feel for each other, that friendship so special they give it a special word. "He's me *marrah*," they'll say. Or "I worked *marrahs* with him ten years past." The word means more than *workmate* or *friend*. It has in it mutuality, humour, dependability and trust; it has shared history and the woven texture of experience.

Like marriage.

Joe'll not like me talking like this, because that's the thing they never do. Talk about it.

You see a cartoon-shadow of this special feeling when there's some documentary on the telly about, say, football fans. Here are these big butch men, some with broad shoulders and beer-bellies, some with narrow sharp faces, drawing hard on a fag, waxing sentimental about their mates or their team, using playground pet-names like Madda, Gazza, Smiler, Chalky, Tommo: the naming a signal of intimacy, real or imagined. This pet-naming's a thing, as far as I can tell, the women don't do.

Not in my experience.

Before the final closure of the last pit, some of the men moved, in a kind of boot-dance dance from pit to pit, as one by one they closed. Refusing the Judas coin, they kept working underground to the last. Joe was one of these. He had this love-hate relationship with the pit. Uncle and two grandfathers killed, but loved it, see. Loved the veins of the earth.

I didn't think much of it when he came home and announced the first move, from Singleton to Maryfield Pit. I put his dinner in front of him and looked absently at his curls through the steam, wondering whether there'd be enough for him. The only thing we quarrel about really is food. He has the appetite of a wolf: there's no filling him. Sometimes, if I give him bought fast food or his plate seems short, he erupts like some great volcano. In my mother's generation I might have got a clout for it, but things are different nowadays.

He sits alongside me watching the television documentaries about battered women.

And I'm sure it makes him think.

Passion / 95

". . . Few of us transferred to Maryfield. That is, if we want to go." He munched away. As usual he talked without really looking at me. Now don't think that worries me. I'm used to it. He thinks the world of me in his own way.

He wiped his mouth with the back of his hand. "You'll remember Maryfield?"

My fork stayed poised. "Maryfield?"

"There was an accident. Seventy-odd men killed there in an explosion. Mebbe seven year ago. Just walled'm up. Never got nowhere near'm." His eyes were on me now. Cool. Grey.

I shivered.

"Not that it makes any difference. Good coal there at Maryfield. Deep seams. It's not on any list." He put his knife and fork together and sat back, forcing his chair on to two legs.

"As far as you know, it's not on any list," I said, biting my lips on pleas for him to come out of the pit: to take the money and try the factories for work, or open a little shop or . . . I had tried pleading before, and he had laughed in my face telling me to mind my own business.

Later that night he kicked a ball about a bit with Patrick and Sean, then sat down and read his paper from front to back: every word, every article-for-sale, every house-for-sale, every birth, every marriage, every death. Then he covered his curls with his oldest cap and went down to the allotment to feed the livestock, just like his dad before him and his dad before that. They've always had allotments in that family.

Joe's an old-fashioned kind of lad, never been to a disco, even before I met him. Just the garden and the pit. The other girls thought I was crazy, going with a lad who'd never even been to a dance. I liked it then. Saw it as steady and reliable. And he was big and really good-looking, then.

Except for a Saturday night he wasn't even interested in the Club . . . Always the allotment. He spends such a long time down there. Maybe the fresh air and the animals are a good change from the pit. From me.

Joe's move to Maryfield didn't make much difference in the end. He had to set out for work sooner, and got back a bit later. He was a bit hungrier and my supermarket bills went up. He sold a couple of pigs and bought a breeding sow. Breeding! I told him he needn't bring his runts down here. I like the house nice and he knows that.

When he's been to the club with his friend Theo on a Saturday night, Joe and me do the usual thing. He's not too pushy but he does like it on a Saturday night. Nothing fancy, mind. You see queer antics on films nowadays. Even on telly. They seem to make a meal of the whole thing. Far-fetched, I think. I couldn't be bothered myself. Joe once said to "turn over, try it that way . . ." and I said no fear, this way's bad enough. So he didn't bother.

Joe's friend, Theo, his marrah, shares the allotment and the stock with him. They've been friends since they were born. Their mothers had been friends; they danced together round their handbags at the Variety Dance Hall; before his mother met his father and stopped going out all together. Theo and Joe *worked marrahs* for the first ten years before Theo, being sensible, got out of the pit and got a factory job.

Theo comes to the house sometimes. He's no bother. Sometimes when he's here, neither of them say much, just look at the telly with a word for each other now and again. Sometimes they clatter on twenty to the dozen, battling to get their own way in much-repeated arguments. It might be the pigs, or the council tax or the bloody Prime Minister.

I tell you what, sometimes those two just about set the world to right.

I just make the sandwiches, maybe a nice bit of pork or ham, and knit and watch the telly turned down low. Their talk dissolves into one long stream to me. A lot about nothing really.

They had this do about a breeding sow. It was 'pigging' but there was a bit of bother. Clucking around, they were, like a pair of old hens. In the end they decided to sit with her in shifts, so the poor dear wouldn't feel too lonely. Oh, I know the pigs are valuable, but if you ask me there's something very motherly about the way those two look to their stock. Like little lasses playing with their dolls. Joe's never motherly about his own children. I'll tell you that. Never saw him for dust when I was having the boys.

Anyhow, the sow survived and there were ten more hungry squealing mouths to feed. So Joe went out before work to feed the stock and would have the fire on for me before I got up.

One night he came back very late after feeding the pigs. "What happened?" I asked.

"Theo didn't turn up," he growled. "An' the sow's rolled on one of her young'ns."

Passion / 97

His dinner was dry and looked shrunken on the plate. He pushed it away. "I cannot eat that."

I pushed it back towards him. "Not my fault you were late, Joe. Blame Theo."

He flung the plate in my direction and I could feel the breeze as it passed my ear. The children cried and I swept them up to bed then went to bed myself. I could hear Joe scrounging around in the kitchen.

You wouldn't believe the mess, the tip, that greeted me in the kitchen the next morning: bread out of its wrapper, beans spilled, congealed on the surface unit.

As the winter came in, Joe's journey through the icy dark to and from work became more treacherous. I watched the weather on the telly and through the window, imagining him struggling to get our old car away, maybe catching a few of the lads to give him a push. I started scanning the paper, to see if there were jobs nearer at hand. Something to suit him. But in my heart I knew I wouldn't get him away from the pit. I knew that one day he'd have to change, because the pit would go from beneath him. Only then would he find something else.

I listened to the saga of despair about the pit closures with a kind of dual mind. On the one hand I knew that Joe would be lost without the pit. On the other hand the last thing I want for my boys is that life in the pit. The life that sucks you away from your family and only leaves you available for your *marrahs*.

One night when the weather was still cold and the snow was still lying, a slushy shadow of a crystal fall, Joe came home on time. I'd made a really good dinner that night: leek puddings and steak and kidney with that little touch of garlic that even Joe liked now The boys had their dinner and were upstairs playing with their computer, an anticipated Christmas present.

Joe ate three mouthfuls and pushed his plate away, folding his lips tight together.

"What's the matter with it?" I know my voice was sharp.

"The dinner? Nothing, Nance. Looks pretty good. To tell you the truth I'm not that hungry."

"Are you feeling bad or something?"

"No. I'm fine. Honest."

I had to be satisfied with this, but I was really mad. I'd taken that much time and trouble for him. I stared at him over my cup.

He looked all right. A bit red and weather-beaten, but he's always like that.

He got down from the table and went up to talk at the kids. He even saw them into bed and tucked them in. I couldn't remember when he's done that, last. I could hear him up there, talking away to them.

When he came back down I had everything neat and tidy. I got my knitting bag and sat down in the chair by the fire. He lay himself full length on the couch and closed his eyes.

"You're not going down to feed the pigs, Joe?"

"Theo said he would, tonight. He's dropping by, after." Joe spoke without opening his eyes.

I leaned over and turned on the television.

Theo came just as Coronation Street was starting, so I turned the sound down low. Theo's taller and heavier than Joe. A nice sort of man. He smiles when he talks to you and looks you in the eye. He laughs at your jokes. When he's in the house the air is lighter, the laughter easier. Women like him, but no-one's managed to snaffle him yet. Joe says he's too light on his feet for that. Even the kids like him, and they're both reserved and a bit cautious like their dad.

Theo cocked his head at the sleeping Joe. "That idle sod been asleep long?"

"An hour, maybe. Sommat up with him, I think. Wouldn't eat his tea and that's not him."

Theo's grimaced. "Thought sommat was up when he called to ask me to feed. Wouldn't miss feeding usually. Half the time he's taken my turn."

I went into the kitchen to make Theo a cup of tea. Measuring the water into the jug kettle I wondered if he were still going with Janie. I liked her. But he has this habit of playing away, has Theo, then letting the girl find out, so she would finish with him.

I could hear voices, so I put out an extra pot for Joe. Plenty of sugar.

Theo was reporting on the animals, then went on to tell the tale of a fight he'd got into at work. No mention of a reason, but it would be something about a woman. They never talked of women, those two.

When I took the tray in, Joe was sitting up, quite relaxed. They murmured away while my needles clicked. They had turned off the television and there was a nice quietness about the place. Then my ears hooked onto what Joe was actually saying. ". . . down this way, on me own, to do me check . . . pitch black, you see. No light but me own beaming down through the black. You know what it's like, Theo . . . Black."

Theo nodded. "Black," he said. "I hated it, meself."

"Well I musta lost me bearings 'cause I turned on this curve an' I came to this blank wall. I knew straight away it was where they walled it up after the explosion. I knew but I can't say I was bothered, like." He leaned towards Theo, elbows on knees, cup in hand. "Anyway, you turn right along there and as I turned the corner my beam passed over this wall facing, an' facin' me there was this man, a giant, taller than any man."

Theo's face had a frown on it and I could hear my own silly intake of breath.

"Me bloody heart, Theo, must a jumped straight out to me ribs! I turns off me lamp an' he vanishes. Not a sound; not a breath. I stand there a full minute then turns it on again. He's still there, this bloody giant of a man.

"What was it, marrah?" said Theo softly.

"A picture, scratched on the wall. Scraps silver chocolate-paper stuck in to the cracks, picking out the lamp, the helmet, the lot. Even the finger nails. So when a light flashes, he's there. This bloody big giant." He paused. "Even the whites of the eyes, Theo. I'm not kidding you. Me heart was beating fit to bust."

"Bloody silly joke," said Theo.

"I don't know." I expressed the thought aloud. "Maybe it was a kind of memorial. You know?"

They both turned, then, to look at me with cold curiosity. I might have just alighted from Mars.

Joe coughed, his cheeks flaring. "May be. You never know." He turned his face away, towards Theo. "Like I said, me heart was fit to bust."

I bent over my knitting, tucking my head close to my chest. As they talked on, tears splodged down onto the wool, making it impossible to work. When I could hear them again they had changed the subject, talking now about jobs cropping up at Theo's factory and the possibility of Joe working there. Joe was listening with keener interest than usual.

But in the end Joe waited until, in its turn, Maryfield Pit was closed. Then, even he had to acknowledge that it was only a matter of time before all the other pits closed. I offered to move away, to be near a surviving pit so he could work there.

But then Joe wouldn't have moved away. Not away from his allotment. From his pigs. From his marrah.

He's happy enough now, working at the factory alongside Theo. They've acquired the next-door allotment and keep hens now as well as pigs. Our boys are at secondary school, where they compete for everything and true comradeship is a thing of the past. I have a part-time job logging orders for a mail-order firm, and am taking Biology and English GCSE at the Tec.

There are no pits anymore: no ghosts of the past, in the flesh or tricked out in silver paper on a wall of coal.

I have to say it very quietly round here, but I think it's a good thing.

The Contributors

Addy Farmer graduated from London University in 1985 and began a career in bookselling. In 1993 she moved north to be with her husband Angus and in June 1994 gave birth to their daughter Freya. Addy plans to become a primary school teacher and to write something funny for children.

Howard Baker, a 47 year old former bookseller, began writing fifteen years ago. He is now a full-time freelance writer and journalist producing material ranging from short stories to magazine features. He has had four novels published and is the holder of two national poetry awards.

Adrian Wilson's surname has been traced back to 1312 in Wakefield, West Yorkshire, which is where he has lived all his life. As a consequence, *Very Acme*, the début travel novel with which he aims to establish his literary name, could be described as less than panoramic. He is the Sports Editor of the *Goole Times & Chronicle*.

Richard J. Hand was born in 1965. He was brought up in Bournemouth, but has drifted steadily northwards in his adult life. Since 1992 he has lectured in Cultural Studies at Humberside University in Hull. Most of his creative work has been in drama.

Johanna Fawkes was born in London in 1952. After working in trade unions and local government, she became a lecturer and now lives in Arnside and teaches in Preston. This is her first published story, written for Lancaster University's MA in Creative Writing. She is currently completing her first novel.

Stuart Allison was born in Hull and is married with a two year old daughter. Recently made redundant, he decided to write full time. BBC Radio 4 broadcast a play years ago but *The Gate* is the first short story success. His first novel, *Charity* is almost ready for submission to an agent.

Ian Smith was born in Doncaster in 1932 and is now devoting himself to writing, having retired from a mainly overseas career.

102 / The Contributors

He is married with two grown up children and lives in Chester. *Jereminsky's Oranges* was influenced by his experiences while working in Central Africa. He is currently working on a novel.

Grace Harvey, originally from the Isle of Man, has lived in the North West for a number of years. Recently retired after a career in Local Government, she is at present writing a novel and is also completing an Honours Degree in Humanities at Leigh College and Bolton Institute.

Stephen G. Holden was born in West Yorkshire in 1953. He was educated at Smithills Grammar School, and Bolton Institute of Higher Education where he graduated in Philosophy. He is married with two children and works for British Telecom and is an active spare-time writer.

Robert Graham lives in Manchester. He co-wrote *Elvis – The Novel* (Grafton, 1984), and wrote *If You Have Five Seconds to Spare* for Contact Theatre in 1989. His stories have appeared in various magazines and on Radio 4. *Carcasses* arose from three months in St. Helens with a missionary organisation.

Gary Webb was born and bred in Blackpool. He is 34 and single and has attended a couple of creative writing classes. This is his first published story.

Kathleen Jones lives near Appleby where she writes and teaches creative writing. Her published work includes *A Glorious Fame* (Bloomsbury, 1988) and *Learning not to be First: The Life of Christina Rossetti* (OUP, 1991). Poetry and short fiction have appeared in a number of magazines and a collection of poetry, *Unwritten Lives,* is to be published in October by Redbeck Press.

Stephen Bohl is 31 years old and lives in Manchester. He has just qualified as a librarian. He worked for two years as a British Rail Guard. At present unemployed, he is currently, completing two novels.

Wendy Robertson was born in South Durham and has spent a large part of her life there. Coming from a family of miners, craftsmen and nurses she spent a chaotic childhood and muddled through to education. Since leaving teaching she has published social/historical novels based in Durham, but is new to short story writing.

The Editors

Beryl Bainbridge was born in 1934. Now living in London, she has written for the stage, film and television as well as novels. She has a weekly column in the *Evening Standard* and was made a Fellow of the Royal Society of Literature in 1978. Among her many publications *The Bottle Factory Outing* (1974) won a Guardian Fiction Award and *Injury Time* (1977) a Whitbread Award. More recently there has been *Forever England* (1986 TV Series), *The Dressmaker* (1973), made into a film in 1987 and *The Birthday Boys* (1991).

David Pownall, a Fellow of the Royal Society of Literature, was born in Liverpool in 1938. He started writing whilst working in the Zambia copperbelt. On returning to England in 1969 he began writing full time, and was playwright-in-residence at the Duke's Playhouse in Lancaster for five years. His novels include *The Sphinx and the Sybarites* (Sinclair Stephenson, 1993) and short stories *My Organic Uncle* (Faber, 1976). His most recent play *Elgar's Rondo* is in the repertoire of the Royal Shakespeare Company.

Shortlist

Shortlist from which the winners were chosen:

Stuart Allison (Driffield)
Howard Atkinson (Sheffield)
Howard Baker (Hull)
Joanne Benford (Lancaster)
Stephen Bohl (Newcastle upon Tyne)
A.J. Derwas (Hull)
Alan Dunn (Penrith)
Addy Farmer (Scunthorpe)
Lowena Faul (Liverpool)
Johanna Fawkes (Arnside)
S. Fielding (Bolton)
Martin Fuller (Wirral)
Lesley Garvey (Leigh)
Robert Graham (Manchester)
Martyn Halsall (Bolton)
Richard J. Hand (Hull)
Grace Harvey (Manchester)
Stephen G. Holden (Bolton)
K. Jones (Appleby)

A.K. King (Wirral)
Ken Lickley (Ilkley)
Richard Longmore (Driffield)
Daithidh Maceochaidh (York)
Michael Noonan (Halifax)
John Rickard (Wallasey)
W.H. Robertson (Bishop Auckland)
Martin Russell (Leeds)
Ian Smith (Chester)
J.D. Taylor (Driffield)
Helen Tookey (Sheffield)
Monica Tracey (Newcastle upon Tyne)
M.B. Wallace (Manchester)
Diane Waters (Sheffield)
Gary Webb (Blackpool)
Adrian Wilson (Wakefield)
John Winrow (Bolton)